Love Never Dies!

Copyright © 2015 by Ophelia Gayle.

All rights reserved. No part of this publication may be reproduced, distributed, or transmitted in any form or by any means, including photocopying, recording, or other electronic or mechanical methods, without the prior written permission of the publisher, except in the case of brief quotations embodied in critical reviews and certain other noncommercial uses permitted by copyright law. For permission requests, write to the publisher, addressed "Attention: Permissions Coordinator," at the address below.

BookVenture Publishing LLC
1000 Country Lane Ste 300
Ishpeming MI 49849
www.bookventure.com
Hotline: 1(877) 276-9751
Fax: 1(877) 864-1686

Ordering Information:
Quantity sales. Special discounts are available on quantity purchases by corporations, associations, and others. For details, contact the publisher at the address above.

Printed in the United States of America

Library of Congress Control Number:		2015949527
ISBN-13:	Softcover	978-1-943265-59-6
	Hardcover	978-1-944014-00-1
	Pdf	978-1-943265-60-2
	ePub	978-1-943265-62-6
	Kindle	978-1-943265-61-9

Rev. date: 08/31/2015

Disclaimer

This publication is designed to provide accurate and personal experience information in regard to the subject matter covered. It is sold with the understanding that the author, contributors, publisher are not engaged in rendering counseling or other professional services. If counseling advice or other expert assistance is required, the services of a competent professional person should be sought out.

Love Never Dies!

Ophelia Gayle

I dedicate this book to Zoe (*Life*).

MOST OF MY aspirations and/or inspirations are born from my dreams; hence, this novel. I've never been one to do a lot of procrastinating, so usually when I get the urge or impulse to do something, I immediately go into "action mode," whether I have the wherewithal to do so or not. I strongly believe that if God has given me the vision, then He'll make allowance for the provision ~ to manifest. That being said, I understand and have a great appreciation for the phrase, "Delay Does Not Mean Denial," and so, I never stop hoping and, therefore, I never stop moving . . . because I never stop dreaming.

While we're embarking on this journey called "*Life*," we're going to be thrown some curve balls, but we all have choices. We can either "catch and/or hold" (*the balls*) or do our best to dodge them.

This is your *Life* for the rest of your *Life* . . .
Make it worth living!

Introduction

I HAD BEEN writing all morning, and was starting to feel a bit lethargic, when I received the call from Allen. He was over-elated about something, but didn't want to tell me over the phone. I tried to partake in his euphoria, but it's hard to get excited about something that you know nothing about, and he insisted that he needed to tell me in person, over an early dinner. Well, that sure changed my disposition, and, at this point, it didn't matter what it was; I was just thrilled that he was finally going to make some time for 'us.' He's been working long, hard hours, and I've been so busy working on my screen writes that we just haven't spent much time together.

Allen works for a successful investment banking firm in Milwaukee, Wisconsin, and I'm a free-lance writer, who works from home. We've been married for three and a half years, but because of our workloads and schedules, we hadn't started our family yet, although we do want children someday. Well, this is the excuse that we tell our family and friends, so they'll get off our backs about it. The truth is, we selfishly want each other, more than rushing into starting a family. Children just didn't fit into our curriculum.

Our passion and desire for one another is erotic and nearly animalistic, at times. Although we appear [on the surface] to be pretty conservative and refined, we are, on occasion, uncontainable when it comes to our sexual endeavors. Just to give a little 'snip' of our indulgence for one another: We were dining at an elegant restaurant, just chatting and intimately enjoying each other's company. Well, the 'intimately' led to touching, the touching led to sexual gestures, and the sexual gestures led to me giving him a nice 'lube job' under the dining table. Of course, no one around us knew what was taking place, because the tablecloth was draped to the floor. When the waitron stopped by to check on us, Allen could barely talk, and all I could hear was him stammering, as he was trying to stay composed as I was putting a nice, wet varnish on his voluminous joystick. It was quite hilarious. Afterwards, he gave me the clear, and I mystically reappeared. This was the surreptitious lifestyle that he and I shared before the changes with his job.

Allen is, without question, the love of my life, for the rest of my life. What I didn't expect was how what he was about to tell me, and its consequences, would affect my life, my thinking, my beliefs, and even my morals.

Chapter One

The Big News!

IT WAS SUCH a beautiful day; the sun was shining, there was a warm breeze, and everything was just wonderful. Because we hadn't gone out for quite some time, I wanted to look refreshed, beautiful, and seductive. I wanted him to look at me like he used to when we were dating - so mesmerized, so passionate, so lovingly - so I decided to pamper myself before our 'hot' date. I went to the spa, received a full body massage, facial, manicure and pedicure, and even stopped by the salon to get a fresh cut and color... all just for him. Looking as cute as a runway model, I took a cab to Allen's job, and there he was standing curbside - so refined, so handsome, so edible, with a wide smile, and all of his pearly whites showing. He opens the door, pays the fare, reaches for my hand, and gently glides me out of the cab. He pulls me close, and says, "Ummm... You look scrumptious!" And then passionately kisses me, right there on the sidewalk, in front of the world - no shame. I'm already panting, and starting to feel a little moist between the thighs. Ohhh... I so love this man... every inch of him.

He says, "Honey, let's take a stroll." I ask, "Well, where are we going?" He gives me this cunning look, and envelops my arm in his, as we start walking. I'm feeling like a school girl and an empress at the same time. A light, warm wind is blowing through my hair, my dress is flowing freely, and the smell of my perfume is captivating. Allen looks like a stallion that's ready to be mounted, and I'm up for the challenge. He stops, unpredictably, and says, "Close your eyes." I close my eyes, and then he says, "Now, open them." There's a gorgeous, black limousine pulling up in front of us. The driver gets out, opens the door, and Allen guides me in. I ask in light tone, "What's this all about, Babe?" He looks over at me and smiles, "It's a surprise." As we're riding, he's holding me close, with his hand up my dress, as he's softly fondling my clit, and playing with my little girl. Whenever I wear a dress around Allen, I know not to wear panties; he loves to play in my kitty-cat. I'm trying to keep a straight face, because the cab driver keeps glancing back at us through his rearview mirror. But, it's not easy when you're being finger-fucked by the one you love. I just want to lean my head back, and sink down into the seat, as I feel myself declining, and ready to climax. He's so amused by me trying to contain myself, and he retreats, but not before seductively licking his fingers. I blow out deeply and sigh, "Wow!" We're both so aroused, and I can see his bulge, however, he's much more composed than I. He just looks over at me and smiles. I'm all sweaty and clammy between the thighs, and need to be relieved. Oh, how I love this man, and I know he loves me. Nothing or no one can come between us… so I thought.

The driver pulls in front of this exclusive restaurant, Alinea, in Chicago. I think to myself, "This must be really be a big surprise for him to hire a limousine, and ride all the way to Chicago, for dinner." How beautiful and distinguished this place is. We're escorted to a private table in the far corner of the room. Well, you can guess where my mind wandered. Allen orders a bottle of their finest champagne, and he straightaway orders our dinner. After that arousing ride, I needed to get to the ladies room to finish what he started, and freshen up a bit. I always keep a little 'something-something' in my purse for times like this. Luckily, no one was in the ladies room at that time, because once the vibration touched my clit, I let out a yelp and moan that was just bursting to get loose. "Ummm..." I return to the table feeling refreshed and satisfied. He smiles at me, and I softly smile back. No words needed, but all is understood.

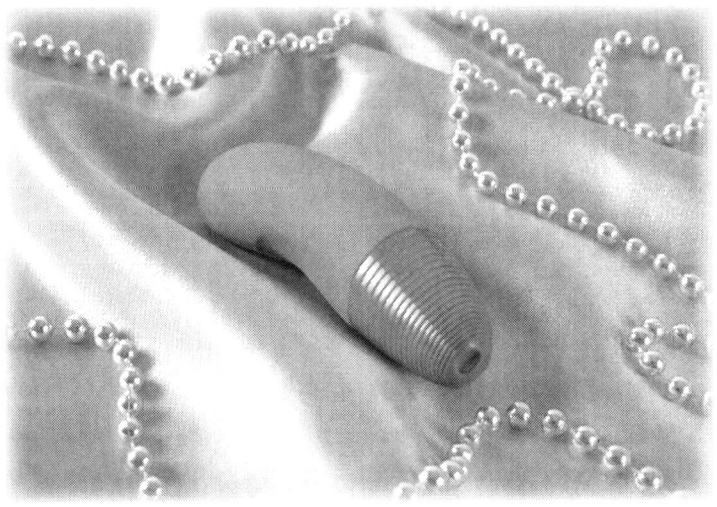

And now I'm so excited that I can't wait to hear this good news. The suspense is killing me, so I impatiently ask, "Allen, what's going on?" He anxiously tells me, "Gayle, Bill (that's his boss) offered me the Partnership position. I was so surprised, that it took me a moment to respond, and then I accepted. I told him, "Yes!" I'm so ecstatic that I get up, go over to his side of the table, hug him around the neck, and I give him a big kiss. "Oh my God! Allen, this is awesome news. Oh Baby! You so deserve it, and it's about time they recognized you for what you're really worth. You've invested and sacrificed lots of time to help make that company the success that it is today." We toast to his big promotion. But then it hits me, and I say to myself, "Oh no! He'll be spending even more time away from home ~ away from me." Suddenly, his disposition changes, and he has this solemn look on his face, "Yeah, you're right, Babe, it is about time they recognized me for all I've done, but I have to be honest with you; this promotion doesn't come without a hitch." I see the overcast coming, and take a deep sigh, "Do I even want to know, Allen?" He continues, "Well, we'll have to move to Chicago." I bellow out, "Chicago! Why Chicago?" ~ forgetting where we were. And then he explains, "That's where the new office is located, and that's where Bill needs me." I'm sitting there stunned and quiet, trying to grasp this, not knowing what to think or feel. I mean, why should we have to just uproot our lives? All the joy and happiness that I was feeling suddenly dissipated, and I move back to my seat. He hesitantly continues, "Gayle, Bill presumptuously knew that I'd say, "Yes," so the company rented us this lovely, fully furnished home in a suburb of Chicago, called Naperville, which is currently being prepped for our arrival. We're only locked into the lease for one year, and if we're not happy afterwards, we can just move. Bill also assures me that you'll be more than pleased." I'm still sitting stunned and speechless, and he continues, "Honey, it's only an hour away, and we're still close enough to our family and friends to visit. I'm sorry, Gayle, but you know this is what I've been working so hard for, and it's an opportunity that I'd be a fool to pass up."

The waitron brings our dinner, and I slowly and quietly begin eating, without looking up at him. I know I need to get myself together, emotionally. Allen speaks up, "Gayle, please trust me on this one. Now, we'll be able to live like we've always dreamed of living." I look up at him, "We already live a very comfortable life, Allen, but I do know and realize that promotion is always good, and so I say to you, my dear, "Congratulations!" Now he jumps up and comes to 'my' side of the table, kisses me, and says "Thank you! Thank you! Thank you!" I playfully push him away. "I guess I was being a little brattish, but the thought of just suddenly relocating our lives, and leaving our families and friends, is a bit overwhelming for me." He's so comforting and humble, "I know, Babe, but it's not like we're leaving the country; it's only an hour away." And he was right; I mean, I sometimes drive an hour, just to shop. But just as I was trying to grasp and accept all of this, he tells me, "Ah, the transition needs to take place within 30 days." I blurt out, "30 days! Are you kidding me?" Now, I'm heated all over again. "How are we supposed to move in 30 days, Allen?" He explains, "Well, the company is purchasing our current home, along with all of our furniture, for more than market value. They're going to use it as a transitional home for relocating families." I just stare at him. He tries to calm and reassure me, "Gayle, we don't have to worry about doing anything, not even packing. The company will take care of everything. All we have to do is move our bodies, and our cars." I sigh, "You know, Allen, it just amazes me how they've just got it all figured out, like they're in control of our lives." He says, "This is once in a lifetime opportunity, Gayle, and I'd be foolish not to seize it." I then ask, "Do we at least get to see it before we move in?" He responds, "By the time they they've finished with everything, it will be time for us to move in." I shake my head, and I take a deep breath, "Well, I guess we'd better get started." He gives me this big smile, grabs my hands across the table, "That's my girl! You won't regret this." I was happy that he was happy, and that's what was important to me.

Chapter Two

It's Moving Day.

WELL, ITS MOVING day, and we wanted to arrive before the movers, to get familiar with the house, so that we're able to direct them with regard to placing our belongings. As we're driving up to the house, we look at each other in astonishment. Could this be the right house? No way! I ask, "Allen would you please verify the address?" He looks at the relocation forms, and with assurance, he says, "Gayle, this is definitely the house." We couldn't believe it. It looks like something out of a luxury homes magazine. The house is absolutely gorgeous. It's picturesque, and it's huge. It has to be at least 11,000 square feet. We hurriedly get out of the car, still looking up at this mansion-like building. Allen anxiously scrambles to find the keys. When he opens the door and we step inside, we both just stand there in amazement. "Oh My God!" was all we could say. We look at each other, and the tears of joy are streaming down our cheeks, as we are awe-stricken. The place was overwhelmingly breathtaking. What were the two of us going to do with this big house? But then as I looked around, I could think of a few things we could do in every room. He picks me up, and swings me around, "Bill told us that we'd be happy, and he was right."

Just then, Allen's cell phone rings. It's Bill calling to see if we liked our new digs. Allen tells him, "Bill, we're speechless! Words can't express how we're feeling at this moment. I think we can manage to get real comfortable here." I hear him laughing, and I shout out, "Bill, I love it! And, yes, you do know my taste. Thank you very much!" Allen talks to Bill for a bit, and then hangs up and says, "Bill told me to tell you that you're welcome, and to thank you for putting up with him having me work so many ridiculous hours. He knows it can't replace the time, but thought it could make up for the abrupt move." I just smile and hold him close, "I love it, and I love you!"

Allen and I are like little children, excitedly rushing from room to room, totally awe-struck. The house was fully furnished. I could never have afforded to buy this type of furniture. The refrigerator and cupboards are full; everything was taken care. Could this be a dream… come true?

The doorbell rings; it's the movers. We run downstairs to let them in. All of our boxes were marked, so all we had to do was show them where the rooms were. While they were unloading, and unpacking our belongings, Allen and I continued to peruse around the house. The walk-out basement was completely finished with an indoor swimming pool, theater room, and exercise room. We open the patio doors and walk out on the Terrace. It was so serene, so secluded, and so private. He couples my face in his hands, kisses me all over my face, and says, "I love you! I love you! I love you! Thank you for making this sacrifice. I promised to make it worth your while." I believe him ~ every word. We embrace as we absorb the sun and mild breeze. Things are so perfect.

It took the movers several hours to finish unloading, and unpacking everything. Allen gave them a big tip, and a big thank you. It's Saturday night, and we're hungry, but just want to eat and relax after this long day. We open a bottle of wine, make a couple sandwiches, and plunge onto the sofa in the family room. Allen turns on the television, and before you know it, we both fall asleep. I was suddenly awakened by a noise coming from the kitchen. I gently get up, trying not to disturb Allen. I walk into the kitchen, look around, and everything appears to be in order… I think. Hum, I must've been dreaming. I turn to go back to the family room, and I hear the noise again. This time, I'm a little afraid, and I scurry to awaken Allen. I whisper, "Allen, Allen; I think I heard something in the kitchen." He's startled, trying to quickly wake up, "What's wrong, Honey?" I repeat, "I think I heard something in the kitchen." He jumps up, and we both tiptoe into the kitchen. We stand there in silence, but we hear nothing. He asks, "What did it sound like?" I answer, "It sounded like a thump." He asked, "A thump?" I whisper, "Yes, a thump!" Then I hear it again. "Allen, did you hear that?" He smacks his lips, "Honey, it's just the sump pump." I say with a chuckle, "Oh, the sump pump!" I sigh with relief, and we both chuckle. He says, "Let's go up to bed; I'm tired."

He undresses and climbs in the bed, but I decide to take a quick shower. While I'm washing myself, I could see his silhouette through the steamed shower glass, just standing there watching me, so I decide to give him an expose'. "Huh, I thought he was so tired."

I crack the shower door, remove the shower head, put it on full pressure, and began to let the water massage my cunt. As I'm coming to a climax, I moan loudly, in hopes that he'd come in and join me, but he doesn't. When I open the shower door, he's not there. I grab my towel, go into the bedroom, and he's sound asleep, practically snoring. I climb into the bed, looking for him to make a move, laugh or something to indicate that he was, indeed, standing there gawking at me. Well, it never happened; he didn't move. Now, I'm feeling a little foolish, I rough the pillow, turn on my side, and fall asleep.

The next morning, he wakes up, and starts kissing and fondling me, and while I was trying to get there, I was still a little puzzled about last night, so I ask him, "Did you come into the bathroom while I was showering?" He says, "Nooo." I say, "Well, I thought I saw you through the shower door watching me." He playfully says, "You wish! Sorry, Honey; it wasn't me, but maybe it was the same person you heard in the kitchen last night." I playfully smack him, "You've got jokes, don't you?" He says, "Honey, I think you're a little paranoid in this big ole' house, but don't worry, you'll get used to it." I look at him and smile, "I know; you're right." I climb on top of him, straddling and grinding on his penis, and he's erect within seconds. He flips me under him, turns me over, props me up on my knees, and slides his ever-so-comforting penis in my beckoning vagina. "Oh-la-la… Good morning sunshine!" I can't get enough of this man. He's so delicious; I could just eat him alive. We lie, nestled in each other's arms until we're sleep again. I feel so wanted, so protected, so loved, and I don't ever want this to end.

A few hours later, the ringing of the phone awakens us. It was my best friend, Ana; I miss her already. Allen jumps up, and chuckles, "Oh boy, I know it's time for me to get up now! Tell Ana hello, and good morning." We both laugh ~ private joke. She always manages to call when we're either about to make love, in the midst of making love, or just after we've made love. It never fails. He showers, get dressed, and heads downstairs.

Ana is excited about the move, and wants to hear all the details. I begin telling her everything about the house, even about the noises and me feeling like someone was watching me in the shower. She laughs and says the same thing that Allen said, about me being a little paranoid. I continue describing the house to her, "Ana, it's absolutely beautiful. It has a double-winding staircase, a gourmet kitchen, 5 bedrooms, 6 1/2 bathrooms, walk-out basement with a pool… I can't wait for you to see it." She's screaming with excitement, and now she has jokes also, "Ahhh, Gayle, what are you going to do with a gourmet kitchen?" I flippantly say, "Ahhh… You'll have to just wait and see. Ha!" She says, "I'm coming out there today; I can't wait to see this place." I inform Allen by way of the Intercom System, "Honey, Ana is on her way." He responds, "Okay, thanks for the warning." We both start laughing. The two of them are always taunting each other, but I know they love each other dearly.

I get up, go into the bathroom, and walk into the shower, but I'm still feeling a little leery after last night, so I peep out to see ~ see what? I don't know what; it was probably just my imagination. Afterwards, I come into the bedroom, open my drawer to get some underwear, and they were all disheveled. Hum, they were just neatly folded yesterday, and I hadn't had a need to go back into that drawer. I look in the other drawers, and everything was still neatly folded. I walk back over to the intercom, "Allen, have you been in my drawers." He chimes back, "No. Why would I need to go in your drawers?" I respond, "Never mind!" Hum… now I'm feeling a bit uneasy, but about what? I take a deep sigh, and continue putting on my clothes, when I suddenly feel a stroke against my hair, as if someone were gently pulling my hair back. I'm startled, and quickly turn my head to see if any windows were left opened, but they weren't. "What the hell was that?" Now, I'm starting to really feel a bit unsettled.

Chapter Three

Who's There?

I HEAD DOWNSTAIRS, and Allen was in the kitchen working on his iPad, and drinking coffee. His legs were spread wide, and "Mister" was calling my name. He stops typing, and looks up at me, while biting his bottom lip. Ohhh, I love it when he does that. I couldn't resist coming over and bestriding him. We begin to kiss passionately, and he picks me up atop of the kitchen island, pulls up my dress, unzips his pants, and swiftly plunges his penis into my opening. And now he's stroking like there's no tomorrow. "Um Um Um... There's nothing like candy for breakfast." He lets out a moan, as he reaches his climax. What a delightful little 'quickie.' How invigorating. We smile at each other and say, "Good morning." We both head for the powder room to wash up before Ana arrives.

As we're sitting at the kitchen table, Allen asks, "Babe, why did you ask if I had been in your drawers?" I explain, "Well, my panties were all disheveled." He says, "Yeah, but that could have happened during the move." I tell him, "I would agree, but I looked in all the drawers after the movers left, and everything was neatly folded, and in place. But you never know, perhaps, I overlooked that particular drawer." All he said was, "Hum." He warmed his coffee, we ate and just talked for a bit. And although we had hardly any housework to do, we just wanted to arrange a few things, more to 'our' liking. I send Allen out to find the nearest grocery store to pick up Ana's favorite beverage ~ red wine. I turn on the music and begin dancing, signing, and rearranging things. I'm so thankful and grateful to God for blessing us so abundantly. Suddenly, the music stops. I go over to the amplifier, and it's turned off. Perhaps, it's a power glitch. I turn it back on, and continue singing, dancing, and rearranging things. There must be something wrong with the amp; maybe there's a shortage, because it goes off again. I go over and turn it back on again, but as soon as I walk away, the music stops again. This time, I'm a little uneasy, and I stand in silence, with my arms folded, wondering what's going on. I quickly rush over to my phone, and call Allen. He answers, "Allen, is there is anything wrong with the amplifier?" He says, "No, it's a newer unit." I tell him, "It keeps cutting off." He says, "Hum, that's strange; that shouldn't be happening. I'll look at it when I get back home." I hang up, but I'm still feeling a little vulnerable, and I'm no longer in the mood to sing or dance, so I sit down and begin mystifyingly looking around the room. I just have this eerie feeling, but I'm not sure why.

I get up and walk around this beautiful home, not believing that its ours. As I start out on the Terrace, I feel something caress one of my breasts. I impulsively grab my breast, and start looking around frantically. I'm a little frightened, and I turn and run back into the house. As I turn the corner, I run into Allen, who scares me even more. He sees that I'm a bit shaken, immediately puts the grocery bags down, grabs me, and frantically asks, "Gayle, what's wrong?" I shout, "Allen something just caressed my breast! Honey, something is in this house!" He looks at me, and just starts laughing uncontrollably. I mean he's in hysterics. Of course, I don't' think it's so funny. He says, "I apologize for laughing, but Honey, listen to what you're saying. You're being a bit irrational." I shout, "Irrational! Irrational! Did you say that I'm being irrational? He says, "Look around! Do you see anyone else in here, but us? Maybe it was the wind." I blurt out, "Allen, I know when I've been touched!" He walks away from me, shaking his head, and giggling. Now, I'm getting a little upset because, not only is he not listening to me, he's making light of my feelings, and mocking me. I feel that he should, at least, give me some type of reassurance and consolation, especially since we made this big move because of him. I was perfectly okay at our old home. I'm shaking my head, and talking to myself between my teeth, "The nerve!"

The doorbell rings; I know its Ana. I take a deep breath to calm myself, and I go into the powder room to regroup. I hear Allen greeting Ana, and I hear her "Ohhhh's and Ahhh's" as she enters the foyer area. She asks, "Where's Gayle?" He mockingly tells her, "She's in here somewhere, looking for the person who grabbed her breast." I hear them both laughing, and as I walk out of the powder room, I give him a stern look. Ana asks, "Did I walk in on something?" I embrace her tightly, give her a half-smile, clutch her by the arm, and walk away from Allen. "No, Ana, you didn't. I'm so glad that you came."

I give her a tour of the house, and she is just 'over-the-top' ecstatic for me. We walk out on the Terrace, and Allen comes out with two glasses of wine. When he hands me my glass, he says, "I'm sorry Gayle. I didn't mean to upset you." I give him a smug look, and he retreats back into the house. Ana giggles, "What's going on with you two?" I tell her everything that's been going on, and the eerie feeling that I'm getting. She gives me this blank stare, and then she bursts out with laughter. I stare at her in disbelief, take a few sips of wine, and wait for her to finish laughing. She sees that it's not so funny to me, and abruptly stops laughing. She says, "Girl, I'm not laughing at you; I'm laughing at what you just told me. You're nuts!" She didn't know what else to say, so she picks up her wine, and gulps it down. I mean, she could have shown a little empathy or, at least, try to pretend to show some concern - being my best friend and all. Then she hesitantly asks, "Gayle, are you still taking those sleeping pills? You know you could be experiencing some of its side effects." Ana knows that sometimes when I have a hard time falling asleep, I may take a couple sleeping pills. I've never told Allen about this because, I didn't want to hear his mouth about addictions, and so forth. I tell her, "No, Ana, I haven't been taking any sleeping pills lately." I felt as though she were patronizing me, so I played along with her. "You know, Ana, you and Allen may have a point. Maybe I am a bit uneasy with the move, this big house, and just being in unfamiliar territory." She says, "Don't worry girl, you'll be alright once you get used to the place. Come this time next month, you'll be laughing about it too." I smile and say, "You know what? I think you're right!" We toast to the new house.

Ana stayed for a few more hours, but had to make her way back to Milwaukee to prepare for work the following day. Allen and I walked her to her car, gave big hugs and kisses, and thanked her for coming out. I was glad that she had come, but at the same time, I was glad that she was leaving. I needed some time to myself. I needed to reassess my feelings... about everything. Could I be over-reacting? Why am I so emotional these days? But, hell, I ought to know when I feel something touching my breasts, especially because of how sensitive they are. I may be a lot of things, but I'm not imagining anything.

Allen and I walk back into the house, and he shouts, "Let's go swimming!" I shout back, "Who hooo! That sounds good to me!" As we're sprinting downstairs, we strip off our clothes, until we're butt naked, and we race and jump into the pool, like little children. At first it was all play, and then Allen decides that he wants to do some laps. So, I choose to sit on the pool ledge, and watch his beautiful body as he glides through the water. As I'm looking, I notice what looks like someone else swimming next to him. I say to myself, "Naaa… It couldn't be." I lean closer, and I swear it looks like someone is swimming next to him. Suddenly, Allen goes under the water, but he's not resurfacing, and I'm a little concerned. I yell out to him, "Allen, what are you doing?" I get up, turn on the bright lights, and run back over to the pool. His head, and then his arm pops up out of the water.

He's gasping for air, and coughing uncontrollably. He slowly swims to the rim of the pool, and as he climbing out, he slips, and is back under the water again. He's kicking, his arms are swinging, and I can see fright in his eyes. It was like he was drowning. I quickly dive into the water, grab him, and help pull him back to the surface. He's gasping for air, coughing, and breathing heavily. I ask, "Allen, what happened?" He says, "I don't know, but it felt like I was being pulled and held under the water." I say, "What! That's impossible, Allen, you're the only one in the water."

We both get out of the pool, and look mysteriously back into the water. We look at each other, and shake our heads. I hunch my shoulders and say, "Nope! No one else is in there." He says, "You know, Gayle, it's been a while since I've swam; I guess I'm a bit rusty." I try to lighted his mood, "Well, my dear, practice makes perfect, and we've got plenty time to practice, right here at home. Are you okay?" He's coughing a little, but says, "I'm okay, but that was a little scary. Suppose you weren't home, and this happened." I tell him, "Well, I am home, and everything is fine." I ask sarcastically, "Ah, did you say that it felt like someone was pulling and holding you under the water?" He knows where I'm going with this, and gives me this 'look' and says, "I'm hungry, let's go up and find something to eat." We dry off, find our clothes, head upstairs, and make a couple sandwiches. We cuddle on the sofa, and watch a movie. After the movie, he says, "Honey, I'm tired and a little drained from the pool; I'm going to turn in. I've got to be at the office early tomorrow morning." I say, "Oh no! You're not leaving me down here alone." We make our way up to the bedroom, get a nice 'quickie,' and drift off to sleep.

Chapter Four

The Ultimate Climax . . . Bathing in Glory

I T'S MONDAY MORNING. I wake up around 7:30 a.m., and roll over onto a note from Allen, "You looked like Sleeping Beauty, and I didn't want to wake you. I'll call you later. Call me if you need me. I love you! Smooches!" I sit up, stretch and smile. I'm so happy about his new job as Partner. This was another unexpected, but well-deserved blessing. Although he has his flaws, as we all do, he is the greatest, and I couldn't have asked for a better person to spend the rest of my life with.

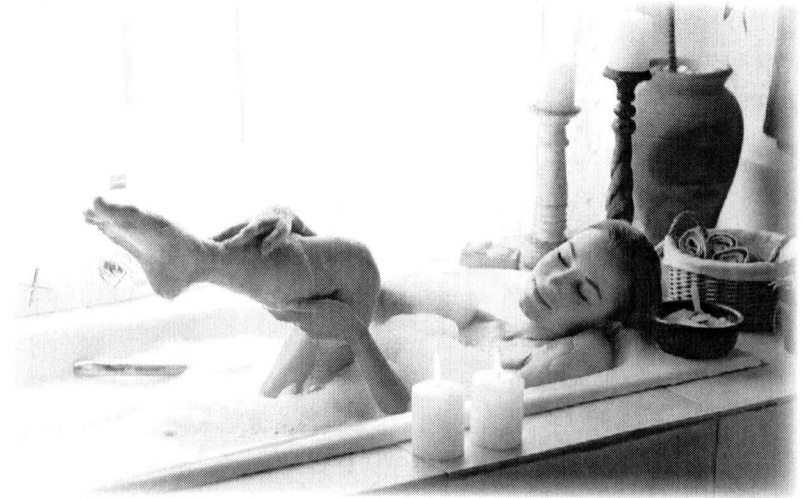

I decide to take a nice, relaxing, and hot bubble bath before I begin writing again - to clear my head, and my thoughts. I recline in the water, close my eyes, and just relax. I find myself drifting off to sleep. How wonderful. How peaceful. How needed. I didn't realize how mentally exhausted I was, as I'm falling into this deep, tranquil-like sleep. Something is enticingly happening to my body. I'm asleep, but I'm moaning, almost to a yowl. I've never felt this aroused in my life. My clitoris is being fondled in a manner in which I'm just not accustomed. It's almost unnatural, but in a very, very good way. I'm so stimulated that my body is quivering, and the orgasms are coming one behind the other. What kind of dream is this? Whatever it is, I don't want to be awakened from it. Instinctively, I spread my legs wider and wider, as I lift them over the sides of the tub. I want more of it. I grab my vagina, and I feel this strong hand, but who's hand? Allen is at work. Oh My Goodness! I feel like I'm about to explode. I'm breathing heavily. Oh My Goodness! Oh My Goodness! Suddenly, I feel this huge penis thrust deeply into my cunt. I breathe out, "Ah... Ahh... Ahhh!" I reach down to grab it, but it's moving ever so smoothly, and I can't get a grip on this slippery bludgeon. What is this? I can't hold it any longer, but I'm not ready for it to stop. I'm breathing and panting heavily, pulling him closer and closer, deeper and deeper. I feel this strong, muscular body just tantalizing my entire being. I succumb, as I've lost all control. My eyes roll to the back of my head, and I let out the loudest screech that I've ever released in my life. I collapse, and lie back in the water, trying to regain composure, but I can barely breathe. My heart is beating fast, and I'm dazed an awe-struck. "What the hell kind of dream was that?"

Whoa! I've never felt anything like this. I lie quietly in a stupor for several minutes until my body calms. I slowly open my eyes, and look around the room, eyes moving to and fro. I'm calm and composed. I slowly get up out of the tub, and wrap myself in the bath towel. I walk over to the mirror, and just stare at myself. My eye makeup is smeared, and my hair is all disheveled. I've never experienced anything like this; it felt so real. I open the towel, and reach down to touch my vagina. My lips were swollen, and there's secretion running from my vagina onto my thighs. It's evident that there was a sexual encounter, and some type of orgasmic occurrence. I let out a deep sigh, "What kind of dream was that?" I'm trying to comprehend, but it's too deep for me, and I can't. I want to soak all of this in. It felt so real. If felt so right. I close my eyes trying to replay the feelings in my head. I say to myself, "Okay! Okay! Okay! Get yourself together." Hum, I need to drift off like that more often. As I'm putting on my clothes and makeup, I can't stop thinking about it. Darn it, I took a relaxing bath to clear my head. Now, my head is clogged for sure.

I go downstairs to my office to work on a screenplay that I've started, but I can't seem to get it together. I definitely have what's called writer's block. Oh well… I go to the kitchen, pour myself a bowl of cereal, and turn on the television. It's the same ole' negative stuff, so I turn it off, and walk out on the Terrace, while eating my cereal. I can't shake this feeling. This is something I would normally share with Ana, but I'm not so sure if that's the right thing to do right now. I'm feeling pretty darn good, so I decide to go out to get some air, and just kind of learn the area. Maybe, I'll go shopping. Yeah, shopping sounds good. I search the Internet for the nearest mall, library, grocery stores, and whatever else is in close proximity, and I head out.

A few hours pass, and I realize that I hadn't heard from Allen all day, so I decide to call him. I didn't really want anything; I was just missing him, and wanted to hear his voice, and see how things were going on his first day as Partner. He was happy to hear from me, and was already packing up to come home. He had been interviewing Investment Bankers for the new office, and pretty much just getting acclimated to the new environment. He wants to dine out this evening, and he asks me to put on something cute. Hum... I guess I can manage that. I rush home, and hide all the evidence of over-shopping, and prepare to go out with my baby.

I hear him calling me from the bottom of the staircase, "Hey Honey, I'm home." I appear at the top of the staircase, looking absolutely salacious. "Hey Baby!" in my seductive voice. He's mooning over me, as he's walking up the stairs. He says, "You look lovely," as he runs his hands under my dress, and up my thighs. I slap his hands, and tell him, "No! No! No! Naughty boy; we're on our way out to dinner, remember?" I give him a sly smile, and a hardy kiss. Lord knows that I'm not mentally ready for him. I'm still pondering on the expedition that took place earlier in the bathtub; and besides, my lips are still a little swollen, and I need those babies to lie down. He says, "You shouldn't be so damn irresistible." He gives me a little peck on the lips, and goes into the bedroom to freshen up. I hear him calling for a cab to pick us up in 20 minutes. I ask, "Why did you call for a cab?" He says, "I didn't feel like driving around, trying to find our way to a restaurant. I know the cab drivers know exactly where to go." I nod in agreement, "You're so smart. That's a great idea. I'll meet you downstairs."

As I'm walking down the stairs, I hear someone whispering softly ~ as soft as the wind, "Gayle, you look absolutely stunning." I turn to look back up the stairs, hoping to see Allen standing there, but he wasn't. I then feel the gentlest touch on my cheek and neck. I touch my face, look around, but nothing or no one is there. I stand still, and ask in a whisper, "Who's there?" Silly me, what do I mean, "Who's there?" Like I really expect someone to answer me. I shake my head, and hesitantly continue to walk into the foyer area. I look out the door, and see the cab driver waiting for us. Just then, Allen comes walking down the stairs. We walk out together.

He holds me close, as we were riding to the restaurant. I deliberately cross my legs, so he wouldn't start playing around with my little girl. She wasn't ready for him just yet. I was pretty quiet, as I couldn't stop thinking about all that I've been encountering since we've moved into this house. However, I dare not mention anything to Allen, or to Ana, for that matter.

I can't seem to get my mind off the dream I had while in the bathtub. It felt so real, and this is what's so perplexing to me. How could a dream feel so literal, so physical? I'm a little vexed because I can't say anything to Allen about this; he already thinks I'm a nymphomaniac, although he's just as hypersexual as I am.

Chapter Five

I'm Trying to Tell You Someone Else Is Here!

THE CAB DRIVER made a great restaurant suggestion. The place was lovely, the food and the service were excellent, and we were very pleased. The evening was quite enjoyable. It felt like we were making up for lost time. After dinner, the concierge hails us a cab, and we head home. It seems like a long drive, but we finally make it home. Allen walks over to the bar and pours two glasses of wine. I tell him, "Honey, I'll be right back; I'd like to change into something a little more comfortable." He says, "Okay, but come here first." I walk over to him, he grabs the back of my head, gives me a long, deep kiss, sighs with gratification, and says, "I love you, girl!" I smile, and make my way up the stairs.

I change into a comfortable evening frock, and as I'm combing my hair in the mirror, I feel something brushing against me, and lifting my gown. I'm thinking that it must be a little static cling, so I gently shake and pull it back down, and make my way back to my man. Then, I hear someone softly calling my name, "Sweet Gayle." I turn quickly, look around, and I shout out in a whisper, "I hear you! Who are you?" I feel a gentle clutch on my arm, and he says, "I want you." I gasp, "What!"

I frantically run down the stairs calling out, "Allen! Allen!" Allen rushes to over, and meets me at the bottom of the stairs, "What's wrong, Gayle!" I'm breathing heavily, shaking, and trying to tell him, "Allen, I heard someone calling my name, and I think he even touched me!" I'm shaking and crying hysterically. Now, he's in hysterics, "What! Who?" I'm trying to tell him, but he's unable to understand my stammering, so he runs upstairs into our bedroom, and then into the other rooms, frantically looking for this intruder. As he's walking back down the stairs toward me, his shoulders are boosted, and he's shaking his head, as if to say, "I didn't see anyone." He pulls me close, and asks, "Who was it? Did you see his face? What did he look like? All the windows are locked, and I checked every room, even the closets, and under the beds, but I did not see anyone, Gayle." Feeling disconcerted, I respond, "Allen, I didn't see anyone either; I just heard him, and I felt him." Now, he's looking at me with his head cocked, and he's batting his eyes, like, "Are you kidding me?" Then he asks, "You felt him? What do you mean, you felt him?" I respond, "Well, he lifted my gown, rubbed my face and neck, and he said that he wanted me."

Allen's just standing there, giving me this perplexed look, like I'm crazy or something. He sighs and asks, "So what you're telling me is that someone got close enough to you to lift your gown, rub your face and neck, and tell you that he wants you, but you didn't see him?" I tell him, "Yes! That's exactly what I'm telling you." He inhales and exhales deeply, "Okay, Gayle, just relax." He leads me to the bar, puts a drink in my hand, and tells me to take a gulp. He picks up the bottle, walks me over to the sofa in the family room, and sits me down. I take a few more gulps of wine, and he takes the glass from me, and asks calmly, "Now, tell me what happened one more time."

I look him in the eyes, and repeat the story, but this time I'm more serene. I even tell him about the dream that now, I'm not so sure if it were actually dream. He's quiet, and I can't help but feel as though he's scrutinizing me. He scratches his head and slowly asks, "Are you taking any kind of medication, other than those sleeping pills? I mean, could you be hallucinating from something, perhaps having a reaction to some medication?" Whoa! How did he know about the sleeping pills? I ask him, "Allen, how did you know about the sleeping pills? And, for your information, I'm not taking any other medication." He responds, "I found them a while back, but never questioned you about them, because I presumed that you must've needed them."

I try to suppress the tears that are welling up in my ducts, but they manage to escape and roll down my cheeks. I'm feeling a little humiliated, but I'm trying to stay calm. "Allen, I know this sounds weird, but I'm not crazy, losing my mind, or having a reaction to any sleeping pills, or any other medication. I know what I heard, and I know what I felt. I'm asking you to please believe me. Allen, something is in this house, and it's alive." He bellows out, "Like what, Gayle? Like who, Gayle?" I grit my teeth, "I don't what!" Now, I'm getting a little defiant, because there he goes again, debasing my feelings. When he hears the tone in my voice, he alters his attitude, "Gayle, I don't mean to make light of the situation, but put yourself in my shoes, and tell me what you'd think. You're hearing noises, someone's calling your name, telling you he wants you, touching your breast, face, and neck, and now you're saying that he fondled your pussy while you were bathing. But, you don't know him, and you can't see him." I nod and confirm, "Yes!" He shouts out, "Come onnn… What do you want me to say? What am I supposed to think?" I sit quietly, looking up at the ceiling. I take a few deeps breaths and say, "You're right; I would probably think you're crazy." He pulls me into his arms, holds me close, and we finish off the bottle of wine.

We're pretty toasted, and rather exhausted ~ mentally. We head upstairs, and when Allen gets to the bedroom door, he peeps his head in, and jokingly shouts, "You whooo, are you in there? You'd better leave my wife alone or you're going to have to deal with me." He starts laughing, but when he looks back at me, of course, I'm not laughing with him. We climb into bed, and Allen instantly falls asleep. He's snoring like a hound, but me, I'm sitting up, looking around the room, trying to listen for any sounds and/or movements. I'm tipsy, tired, and exhausted, but I'm able to finally drift off to sleep.

Sometime during the middle of the night, I feel Allen (at least who I thought was Allen) sucking on my breasts and panting heavily. I mumble, "Allen, I'm really tired; can we resume this in the morning?" I'm so intoxicated, I fall back to sleep, but Mr. Frisky is at it again. I roll over onto my stomach, totally lethargic from the wine. I just want to sleep, but he's not having it. He starts lubricating my anus with his tongue, and then he inserts his finger, gently massaging the hole, over and over, before he penetrates it with his penis. I'm zoned, but I think to myself, "Hum. He hasn't done this is quite some time." He's ever so gentle back there, and I'm totally relaxed, just moving and flexing, as he's working his magic on my ass. I'm moaning and breathing so hard that I can barely contain myself. I let out a yelp, as I release this burst of energy that explodes from my pussy. This gets him more aroused, as I feel his penis swelling, and his strokes increasing. He's moaning and grunting so loud, as if he's about to let out a big one. Suddenly, he howls out like a beast in heat. It was so loud that it woke me up, and I mutter, "Are you okay?" He gently relaxes, lies on my back, and is breathing heavily. He whispers, ever so softly, "I'm okay, Honey. It was just so damn good; thank you." I say in my thoughts, "I don't know what got into him, but that was the best anal sex that I've ever had. It must be the alcohol." He gets up and goes into the bathroom, brings back a warm, wet towel, and begins gently wiping my anal area. Ohhh... It feels so good; he's so thoughtful.

I must've slept very sound because when I woke up, Allen had already left for work. He left a note, "Didn't want to wake you, my sleeping beauty. I'll call you from the office. Love you!" Hum, he didn't even mention anything about what just happened in the middle of the night, and that's all that's on my mind right now. Sometimes, I wonder if anyone else makes love like we do. I know he said that he'd call me later, but I couldn't wait to talk with him, so I call his office, and he answers. I say, "Thank you, Babe." He naively asks, "What are you thanking me for?" I respond. "Hum... like you don't know." He says, "Ohhh... you mean the note." I say, "No silly; not the note! You know very well what I'm talking about." He interjects, "Honey, I'm sorry, and I don't mean to cut you off, but I'm running late for a meeting that's already in progress. I'll call you later. Love you." Hum. I know he's busy, but he could have at least said a little something about what happened. It's not like him not to give me a little dirty talk. Oh well...

Ophelia Gayle

Chapter Six

OMG! ~ I've Been Violated!

I GET DRESSED, and make my way downstairs to the kitchen. I'm in good spirits, and I'm singing and prancing around. I pour myself a glass of orange juice, and suddenly I hear, "Good morning beautiful." I'm terrified, and I drop the glass of orange juice, and shattered glass is everywhere. I back up to the counter, grab a knife from the knife block, and ask in a very trembling voice, "Who are you, and what do you want?" He responds, "There's no need to be afraid of me; I'll never hurt you." I ask again, "Who are you? What do you want? And, why are you here?" He says, "You'll know in due time, and by the way, thank you so much for this yesterday. Oh… and last night. You were so amazing, and you felt so good." I, half-heartedly ask, "Yesterday and last night, what do you mean? What are you saying?" My eyes surge with tears, fearful of the obvious answer? And, he answers, "You know, the amazing love-making between the two of us. It's been quite some time since I've been able to make love like that. You're so soft, yet so meaty, just moving to my every stroke. It felt like I was in ecstasy. I'm just glad that you enjoyed it as much, or even more than I did. Your body was quivering, even after it was over. It made me so happy to see you so satisfied."

I stand there stunned, and in total shock, with tears flowing down, and saturating my face. I'm sobbing, and I shout, "Who are you?" He repeats, "Gayle, please don't be afraid of me." I can feel the vapor of his breath, so close to my face. I'm petrified, and I grab my purse and keys, with the knife still in my hand, and run for the garage door. I'm crying and yelling at him, "Leave me alone!" I can hear him rustling behind me, but I can't see him. He says, "Gayle, I didn't mean to upset you. Please, please stay and talk with me." He grabs my arm, and begs me not to leave. I'm so afraid that I freeze, and my heart is palpitating so fast, like it's about to jump straight out of my chest. I drop the knife, and I'm shaking like a leaf, trying not to pass out. I beg him, "Please don't hurt me; I'll do whatever you want. Just please don't hurt me." His voice is soft and charming, "My desire is not to harm you, Gayle. My desire is to love you like you've never been loved before." He gently releases my arm, and I jet out the garage door, jump in the car, and speed out of the garage.

O.M.G.! I'm crying so hard that I have to pull over and park, to try to gain some composure. I'm breathing hard and crying in disbelief. I knew I wasn't crazy, but who can I possibly tell about this? Now, I know why Allen didn't know what I was talking about; it wasn't him that I was making love to. Oh My God! I repeat, over and over, "This cannot be real!" But, I know it's as real as it gets. I'm trying to find reason, but I can't. I know I should feel like throwing up, but I don't. Why do I not feel like throwing up? This is not natural. I mean, I had sex with a ghost… in my ass, at that. I can't see him, but I can hear and feel him. This is insane! It's really hard for me to phantom this, however, it is what it is. I fucked a ghost! I'm rocking back and forth, trying to get a grip. I take deep breaths, inhaling and exhaling, and then I pause, straighten up, and realize that while this will never make common sense to anyone, it's real. And, I took much pleasure in making love to him, and it was the best love-making that I've ever experienced. Oh My God! I can't believe what I'm saying.

But now my mind is racing, and I'm a curious. Who is he? Why is he in my house? Oh my goodness! I'm in trouble! What should I do? Should I tell Allen? Oh, hell no! Should I tell Ana? Oh, hell to the double-no! I need to talk to someone about this, or I'm going to lose my mind. Lord, please help me! I need to talk to someone more rational than I am right now. Should I tell my sister? Definitely not! She'll tell the whole family, and I'll never live this down. I'd be the laughing stock of the entire family. I've got to talk this thing through. I, reluctantly, decide to call Ana. I pray that I'm making the right decision. Ana answers the phone in her normal, cherry tone, "Hey Girl. What's going on? I haven't heard…" I cut her off in mid-sentence, "Ana, I need to talk with you." She says, "Okay, shoot." I reiterate, "Seriously, Ana; I need to talk with you now, but face to face. Ana, it's really important." She senses the urgency and importance of the call and asks, "Where and when?" I tell her, "I'll come your way." She says, I'm at work, but I'll meet you at my house in an hour."

As I'm driving up to Milwaukee, I can't help but think about this morning. I'm so bewildered that I can't see or think straight. Now, it all adds up. Everything! Everything! I knew I wasn't crazy. The closer I get to Ana's home, the more nervous I am about telling her. Shoot! I should have never called her. Now, I'm shaking with confusion, trying to grasp it all. Could this be real? Yes, of course it's real, but it's not real. I'm certainly not dreaming. Lord, please help me! I beg you.

Chapter Seven

Confiding in My BFF . . .

ANA AND I pull up to her house, and we park around the same time. She's smiling and waving, and I'm trying to reciprocate, but I've got too much on mind to be Ms. Happy-Go-Lucky right now. We both get out of our cars and embrace. I immediately start sobbing, and she holds me very close. You can see the worry in her countenance, and she asks, "What's wrong, Gayle? Are you okay?" I nod, but I'm sobbing so much, that I'm unable to comprehensively speak, so she just continues to hold me, as we walk up to her house. When we enter, she sits me down on the sofa, and with much concern asks, "Did something happened between you and Allen? I finally gain enough composure, "Ana, everything is wonderful between Allen and me." She asks, "Well, then what's wrong? What has you this upset? Is it the new house?" I tell her, "No… Well, sort of." She says, "Huh! What does that mean?" I just look at her and shake my head, as I'm trying to figure out how to tell her 'my' story. Then she slowly says, "Gayle, please talk to me. Are you in trouble?" I calmly tell her, "No, Ana; I'm not in trouble, but then again, yes, I could be. I really don't know where to begin." She gets up, pours wine in two glasses, and hands me one, "Okay Gayle; now just start from the beginning."

I humbly plead with her, "Ana, I beg you to please listen, and don't interrupt or comment until I'm done. And, most of all, please don't judge me." I could see that she's a little offended from her facial expression, but she could also see how dire this is to me. She says, "Gayle, how could you say those words? We've known each other too long, and we're too close for you to even remotely feel insecure about telling me anything. Girl, we've been through too much ~ together!" I close my eyes and sigh deeply, "I know, Ana, but I really don't know where to begin with this." She repeats, "Like I said, Gayle, just start from the beginning." I take a deep breath and begin explaining everything to her, from start to finish. At first, she just stares at me in silence. I'm getting a lot of that lately. Then, she curls her lips, folds her arms, and gives me this empty look, "Gayle, are you trying to tell me that there is a ghost in your house, and you've fucked it." I lower my head, "Ana, I know it sounds crazy, and I don't even understand it. It's really complicated." She blurts out, "No shit, Gayle!" I try to bring in reason, "Listen, Ana, I know this sounds weird, and even spooky, but I know I'm not making this stuff up. At first, I thought I was either hearing things or dreaming, but now I know it's more than that." Then she patronizingly asks, "Are these things happening after you've been drinking." I softly respond, "No, not necessarily." She breathes heavily through her nostrils, gets up, turns her back to me, and finishes her glass of wine. She then turns back towards me and asks, "Have you told Allen about this, and if so, what does he think?" I respond, "Well, I've told him about everything, but the anal sex. And... I did not mentioned that he screwed me in the bathtub; I told him that I was just fondled." She looks at me with her eyes wide, chuckles and shakes her head, "Maybe Allen is working too many hours, and not giving you enough attention. Do you think that you could be vying for more of his attention?" I give her this firm look, "Ana, as long as you've known me, you know that I've never had to vie for Allen's or anyone else's attention – that's the least of my problems, and I think you know that!"

Then she reaches even deeper, and suggests, "Well maybe you should consider seeing a psychiatrist or psychologist, to see what's really going on inside that head of yours." I'm really trying hard not to feel insulted, because I know that this is a hard pill for anyone to swallow. I mean, I'm still trying to wrap my head around it. "Ana, I don't need a doctor right now; I just need a friend." She blurts out, "I am your friend, Gayle, but how do really expect me to believe something so ridiculous? I mean, come onnn… a ghost calling your name, and having sex with you! Gayle, listen to what you're saying to me! Listen to what you're asking me to comprehend!" I concur, "Ana, I completely understand your reaction, as I would probably feel the same way, if our roles were reversed, but you know me. You know I wouldn't just make up something like this. You've got to know that something is going on for me to be this anxious." She pauses, "Yeah, something is going on alright! You need help!" I'm now exasperated, "Ana, I was looking for you to at least try to help me sort this out, and figure out what to do, but all you're trying to do is denigrate me." With indignation, she says, "Denigrate you! Denigrate you! You rush up here, have me leave my job early, meet with you, only to hear you tell me this "out-of-this-world" story about you fucking a ghost – and I'm denigrating you? I don't think so! Gayle, you have my advice; go see a doctor. I'm going back to work!"

I calmly, but disappointedly, rise from the sofa, "You know, Ana, you might be right; maybe I do need to see a doctor." I walk to the door, emotionally broken, "Well, I'd better be getting back to Naperville before the traffic gets too congested. Thanks for listening to my incomprehensible story." She can see the despondency in my gestures, and on my face, but asks me, "Are you having an affair?" I shout, "For goodness-sake, Ana! If I were having an affair, it wouldn't be a problem telling you, of all people; you're my best friend! It's a little deeper than that. I wouldn't have driven an hour to just tell you that. I would have told you something like that over the telephone." She shakes her head, "Well, I wish I had an answer for you, Gayle. My only suggestion is for you to consult with a doctor. This is way beyond my reach, and out of my league. I've got to head back to work." She opens the door, we embrace, and both walk out to our respective vehicles. She'll never know how much I needed her. I'm feeling worst now than when I came. I turn back to her, "Ana, please don't mention any of this to Allen." She says, "I promise I won't." But, I don't know if I believe her.

I'm driving home, and tears are flowing, as I'm trying to grasp this unimaginable situation. I don't know what I was expecting from her; I guess I just needed to unload this heaviness. Even if I did see a doctor, he would treat me like Ana and Allen are treating me, and would, more than likely, try to sedate me, and give me tons of pills. And, I'm not having that, especially because I know what I know, and that is, I'm not crazy. In fact, I'm far from it.

I drive to that same little park, get out of the car, and sit on a bench to ponder a bit. I've decided that I would never tell Allen about the sex incident. He really wouldn't understand, and would think I'm a coo-coo for real. However, the last thing I need is for Ana to call Allen, or anyone else for that matter, and start babbling about my visit to her. Somehow, I needed to quickly pacify and rectify this situation with her. So, I call her, "Hey Ana, I just want you to know that while I was driving back,

I thought long and hard about what you and Allen were both saying to me about the anxiety from the move, and I will take your advice, and consider consulting with a professional. Allen has been working a lot of hours, and maybe I am looking for more of his attention. I'm behaving like an emotional wreck, in hopes that things would change ~ that he'll spend more time…" She interrupts, "Gayle, if you need me to go with you to the doctor's office, I will." Urggg… She gets on my last nerve, but I stay collected and say, "I'll be alright, Ana. I'm just sorry for striking out at you. I know that was pretty heavy stuff that I laid on you. You think I'm PMSing?" She starts laughing, "I think that could be a strong possibility. Is it that time of month?" She laughs, "I'm sorry for upsetting you Gayle. I could have handled the situation a little better, but honestly, I didn't know what to do or what to say. I have to confess though, you did have me a little scared. Let's just forget about it, and move on." I play it off, "I agree, Ana, and thanks for helping me bring clarity to the situation." All was forgiven and forgotten, so she thinks.

Just to change the subject, I say, "Oh Ana, I've decided that I want to have a house-celebration party, and I need your help ~ no gifts, just people, drinks, lots of food, dancing, and fun. What do you think?" Excitedly she says, "I'm onboard. When?" I respond, "Well, how about two Saturdays from now?" She says, "Just tell me what you need, and I'm there." I tell her, "Let me run this by Allen, and I'll call you right back. I know he'll be okay with it, but I want to make sure he's included." We ended the call on an upbeat note. Whew! I think I've got her tamed for now. I immediately call Allen, and tell him about the party plans. He thinks it's a good idea, and said he's on board. He said he'll help wherever he's needed. I called Ana back, "Okay, we've got the green light from Allen. Let's start planning." She's excited.

While my motive was to silence Ana, this was also a good diversion for me. I wasn't quite ready to go home, as I didn't want to face what was obviously waiting there for me. So, I sat in the park for a while, compiling the guests list, and menu for the party. I finally decide to go home. If I can't discuss this with Allen or Ana, then I must face it alone. I've got to confront the inevitable. I'm a little hesitant, but I open the door slowly, hoping he didn't hear me, and I walk into the kitchen. Shoots! I forgot about the mess I left, so I grab the broom and dustpan, sweep up the broken glass, and wipe up the spilled orange juice. There's still no sign of You-Know-Who or You-Know-What. I sit at the kitchen table and begin to make calls, inviting people to the party. I'll also send Evites, but I wanted to give everyone the heads up, and so far, everyone is thrilled. As I'm wrapping up, I, apprehensively, look around to see if there's any sign of movement, and then I hear Allen coming through the garage door. What a relief. I jump up to greet him with hugs and kisses. Thank God he's home. He apologizes for coming home so late, but I didn't care, as long as he came home.

We sit at the island in the kitchen, just laughing and talking, and he, hesitantly asks, "Are you okay after what happened last night?" I tell him, "I'm fine, Allen. I admit that I was probably over-reacting. It's close to that time of month, and I might be a little emotional." He lightly kisses me on my lips, "Its okay, Honey." Then he asks, "By the way, what were you thanking me for when you called this morning?" I smile, "It was for comforting me, and leaving me that nice note. You're such an amazing husband, Allen." He smiles back, "And you're such a wonderful wife, Gayle." I'm feeling so guilty. I feel like I've cheated on him, but I did think I was making love to him, so that couldn't be cheating… could it?

It was more like I was being seduced. I'm trying to convince myself of this, especially since I was so receptive to, 'whoever he is.'

Allen opens the refrigerator, grabs a beer, and is looking for something to snack on. Finding nothing that he really wants, he pops open the beer, begins drinking, and then asks, "How was your day, Honey." I tell him, "Well, I was missing Ana, so I drove up to see her, and you were right, an hour drive isn't so bad." He chuckles, "I told you." I glance over at him, and smile. Then he asks, "Honey, have you been doing any writing lately?" I respond, "I've tried, but I'm still at a stand-still. I'll start up again tomorrow." He nods, we talk about the party a little more, and then he heads toward the Family Room. He turns on the television, and flops down on the sofa. Of course, I join him, as I didn't want to take a chance of being alone, and You-Know-Who decides to show up. Allen abruptly says, "Oh yeah, let me tell you now, before I forget. I have to fly to Denver for few days. I'll be leaving day after tomorrow." I give him a sad look, and he snuggles me close and kisses me, "Don't worry my little princess, I'll be thinking of you the entire time." I look up at him, "And I'll be waiting right here when you return, my knight." We smile at each other, and continue watching television. I'm used to his business trips, but this time was different; things were a lot different. I was, for the first time, a little nervous about being home along, but I dare not tell him about these feelings.

While he's watching the game, I snuggle closer, and drift off to sleep. He makes me feel so safe. After the game ends, he gently wakes me, so we can go up to bed. He decides to take the elevator. We rarely take the elevator, but, I quickly realize what he's up to. He pins me against the wall of the elevator, lifts me up on the rail, pulls my panties to the side, and plunges his cock into my opening. I take in a big gulp of air, as he thrusts himself inside of me. As he's stroking, I'm just making juice. He can feel me pulsating, as I'm about to cum. He's turned on by the grips, and I can feel him swelling inside of me. We both climax, and gently collapse on the elevator floor. We shower together, climb in bed naked, and fall asleep. I wake up a couple hours later, crawl under the blanket, and begin to suck him off. He's moaning, and gently pulling my hair, as he ejaculates in my mouth. I come from under the blankets, and lie on top of him. He thanks me, we kiss, snuggle, and go back to sleep – smiling.

Chapter Eight

I've Succumb . . .
I Can't Fight the Feeling.

ALLEN LEAVES FOR the office, and I'm sitting on my computer, just typing away. Everything is so peaceful and still, and I'm just absorbing it all. I'm about two hours into the manuscript, I'm on a roll, and feeling good about it, when suddenly, I hear someone whispering my name. I, guardedly, stop typing. I don't say a word, but sit fearful and immobile. I mumble under my breath, "Lord, please help me!" This time the voice is closer, as he calls my name once again, "Gayle." I slowly stand, and muster up the nerve to speak back, "I'm not afraid of you! What do you want, and why are you pursuing me?" He replies, "I don't mean to upset you; I'd just like to get to know you." I demand, "Who are you?" He responds in a very self-satisfying tone, "Who I am is irrelevant, at the present." Now he's up close and very personal, and I can feel the warm vapor of his breath brushing against my face. I'm trembling almost uncontrollably, and he speaks ever so softly ~ so ensnaring, "Please don't be afraid of me. I promise I will never harm you." OMG! He touches me! He caresses the side of my face in his palm, tilts my head and whispers, "Just relax, Gayle." I'm so petrified that I feel like I'm about to pass out. He then kisses me on my lips. This sends me into total hysterics; I scream and rush out of the office, stumbling and nearly falling. He grabs me tenderly, to keep me from plummeting on my face. He pleads, "Please, please, don't be afraid of me."

I dash over to the bar, and blurt out to him, "You cannot be real! You've got to be a figment of my imagination! But, I can't conceive why; I'm happy, my life is content, and I have no voids to fill!" He says, "You can try to convince yourself that you don't have any voids to fill, and that's okay with me; that's not why I'm here. I'm here because I live here." I exclaim, "Excuse me! What do you mean, you live here? My husband and I live here, and you're in 'our' home!" He says, "No, you and your husband moved into 'my' home." At this moment, all I want to do is run out of the house again, but it makes no sense to leave; he'll just be here when I return, so I must face this. I try to calm this nervous tension, by pouring myself a strong drink. I'm looking for an escape, and trying to convince myself that this is just a dream, that this could not be real. And, although I know it is very real, I'm deliberately in denial. I quickly guzzle down the drink, pour another one, and guzzle it down also. He's still talking to me, but I'm trying to block him out of my hearing, out of my mind. I pour a third drink, and then a fourth, as I'm chanting, "This this cannot be real! This is not happening again!" I'm heavily intoxicated now, and he's still talking, but I'm trying to ignore what is evident. I cover my ears with the palms of my hands, slowly stammer upstairs to my bedroom, and slam and lock the door. My head is spinning, and I fall across the bed. I'm holding my head, and rocking back and forth. I've had too much to drink, too fast. It feels like the room is rotating, and I just want it to stop. The next thing I know, I feel him get into the bed. But how? With impaired speech,

I ask, "How did you get in here?" He facetiously says, "I've got special keys to every door in this house."

He begins to passionately kiss and suckle my face and neck. I turn every which way, to avoid his advances, but it's hard to control what you can't see. I'm trying to push him away, but the more I push, the more tenderly he gropes. I wrestle and pound on his chest, begging him to stop. His touches are nearly hypnotic, and irresistible. I can't help myself; I give in, and begin to reciprocate, as I'm telling him to stop. I'm behaving like a little hussy. He's so gentle, yet so strong, as he's pulling me closer and closer to him, whispering about how much he loves loving on me. I'm getting overly aroused, as he's fondling my clitoris and vulva areas. It must be the alcohol, but I don't want him to stop. Although my lips are saying stop, my mind is saying please don't stop. He unbuttons my blouse, and I frantically try to assist him, but I'm too plastered. He sucks my breasts, and they're sensitive to his touch. He pulls down my pants and panties and, again, I try to assist. Now, I want him in me, and I want him badly. His tongue and mouth are engulfing my entire vagina area. He then repositions himself, and begins licking my anus. I'm so overtaken, and I beg him again, "Please stop," as I'm coming to a climax. OMG! What about Allen? I'm breathing hard, and hollering out Allen's name, as I'm reaching my peak. He whispers in my ear, "I'm not Allen." He then rises from below, inserts his succulent dick into my pussy, and I scream out with pleasure. I've never felt like this before. What is he? Where did he come from? He then flips me over, massages my anal area, and inserts himself. I toot my ass, as I want all of his cock inside of me. This is too good to be true. I feel like I'm floating, and in another world. I'm thinking to myself, "I'm so sorry Allen; I'm so, so sorry." I feel his penis swelling inside my rectum, as

Ophelia Gayle

he cums. Just the sound of his heavy breathing brings me to another climax ~ just knowing that he's enjoying me so much. I'm now lying in his arms, feeling more than fulfilled. Between him and the alcohol, I'm completely depleted, and I just fold over.

Unbeknownst to me; Allen had come home early, and was calling out for me, but I didn't hear him. I was so busy getting busy with You-Know-Who. He had been watching me make love, and I didn't even know it. The irony of it all is, Allen thinks that I was dreaming about us, because he heard me calling out his name. I feel so mortified.

Allen scares the 'bejeezus' out of me, when out of nowhere, he appears and says, "Ohhh baby! Um… Um… Um… I heard your moans and cries, as I was coming up the stairs, and when I walked into the bedroom, I saw you in rare form. I was about to interrupt and join in, but when I heard you calling out my name, I got so turned on, and so aroused just watching your body tremors that I just laid back on the chaise, and started masturbating." My drunkenness quickly wears, and I look up and faintly smile at him. He continues "I've never seen you so stimulated, and when you screamed out my name, I just let loose, and cum gushed out everywhere. There was no way in hell that I was going to interrupt that dream." I felt both unnerved and remorseful, but I couldn't let him know this, "I sluggishly move my head from side to side, "Mmmm… Allen, you wouldn't believe this dream. I don't know what got into you. I mean, it was like you were a totally different person ~ like someone straight out of a porn movie. You have never made love to me like this before."

Allen climbs onto the bed, and lies next to me, with his penis sticking out of his pants, as hard as a rock. I know what he wants, but I am completely quenched, and I know my little va-jay-jay could not take another ounce of dick ~ not this soon. Now, this was a first for me because Allen and I have been known to go a few rounds before quitting. But this guy... Huh! He's no joke. I mean, I've never been so gratified in all my sexual life... by anyone.

Allen then begins sniffing at me, and gives me this "I-can't-believe-it" look. He sits up, braces himself on his elbows, and probes," Gayle, what have you been drinking? I can't believe that you've been drinking, this early in the day! And, it smells like strong liquor. What's up with that?" Whew, I thought he noticed something else, but all he was talking about was me drinking. What a relief! I respond, "Allen, I know it's early, but I had gotten really frustrated, because I just couldn't seem to get it together. I'm still having writer's block." I couldn't tell him what really happened. But now I have to listen to his counsel, "Gayle, alcohol is not the solution to writer's block. In fact, it could do you more harm than good, in the long run. Please be careful with that; it's not that serious." I nod in agreement, "You're right, Allen." He continues, "Also, I've been calling you. Why didn't you answer your phone?" I apologize, "I'm sorry, Allen. You must've called while I was napping."

I discretely feel around in the bed to see if 'You-Know-Who' is in the bed with us, but thank goodness, he isn't. Oh my goodness! I feel so bad. How could I do this to the man that I so adore? I didn't want him to see the tears streaming down my cheeks, so I hold him close to me, and I tell him, "I'm so glad that you're home, Allen." The truth is, I didn't want to stop feeling what I was feeling, at least not so soon. I want to bask in it ~ to muse over it. But at the same time, I'm feeling so guilt-ridden. Allen is so proud to know that he can make me feel like that ~ even in my dreams. I look over at him and give a light chuckle, and he chuckles with pride. I get up to take a shower, and he asks, "Where are you going, Honey." I say, I'm feeling a bit sticky, and need a shower." He laughs, "I just bet you do."

I cried really hard while in the shower. What have I done? What am I doing? But, although I'm having these feelings, I can't stop thinking about 'him.' Who is this mysterious man? When I step out of the shower, Allen is standing over the basin washing his penis. He says, "I came home early today, because I've got to catch an early flight into Denver in the morning, and I want to spend some time with you, before I leave." I can't believe that I forgot about his business trip. I say, "Oh yeah, I forgot that you were leaving tomorrow." He looks surprised, "How did you forget that?" I reply, "I'm sorry, Allen; I've been so preoccupied lately." Uh Oh… I'm slipping.

We meet downstairs, and I prepare something for us to eat. Allen turns on some soft music, and we're just chit-chatting about any and everything, including the upcoming party. I give him the party details, "Well, so far, we're expecting between 45-50 people, you're responsible for the booze, and between Ana, myself, and the caterer, the food is covered. While you're away, Ana's coming down here, and she and I are going shopping to get a head start on things." He snickers, "Humm… I see you two are back to old habits again ~ shopping, but I also think it would be good for you. I think you could use some 'girl time,' and shopping is always a good distraction." I'm thinking to myself, "In more ways than you could possibly know."

Allen then starts to expound on that 'so-called' dream again. Oh my goodness! I stop him before he can get started. "Allen, it was nothing; it was just a dream." I can never tell him that he wasn't the main character, nor was he even a part of it. He cynically blurts, "Well, from the looks of your body movements, it was a pretty intense dream!" I just look over at him, roll my eyes, and try to play it down. He has this solemn look, "Are you feeling lonely during the days. I mean, it seems like you've been drinking a little more than usual." I grab his face with both hands, and kiss his lips, "Lonely is definitely not an issue for me, nor has it ever been. I love you, and I know you love me. I have no issues with our love-making, or the time we spend, or are not spending together. I'm happy, Honey; It was just a couple drinks, and it was just a dream." He then asks, "Would you please let me know if I'm slacking in any way? My desire is to keep you happy." I smile, "I promise I will, but I am happy, and it's because of you." I feel awful!

Allen goes down to the theater room to watch a movie, and I go to the kitchen to clean up. Mr. Invisible whispers in my ear, "You're good. What a nice cover-up ~ Just a dream, huh!" I whisper and beg him, "Please go away! My husband might hear you." He replies, "Oh, he can't hear me with that television being so loud. So, the hubbie is leaving you for a few days. Well, he need not worry; I'll be right here taking good care of you. You know the saying ~ while the hubbie's away, we'll have more time to play." I beg him again, "Please go away!" Instead, he starts teasing and tickling me, and I start laughing and pushing him away. Allen just happens to come into the kitchen, and he asks, "Honey, are you okay?" I nearly jump out of my skin, "Yes, I'm fine, Honey." He then asks, "What were you doing?" I respond, "Nothing, I was just singing, and thinking about us. Do you need anything?" He says, "No, I just came up to grab a beer." He gives me this puzzled look, and heads back downstairs. I lean on the counter, relieved that he didn't hear me talking to You-Know-Who. Mr. Invisible opens his big mouth again, "Whew! That was close." I tell him, "Shhh, keep your voice down. Do you want Allen to hear you?" He whispers, "No!" I demand, "Okay then, leave me alone! I'll talk with you tomorrow, after Allen leaves." He says, "Okay, okay, I'll leave you alone, but I'm staying right here; I love watching you." I shake my head, "Shhh."

I finish cleaning the kitchen, and head upstairs to bed. Allen is still downstairs in the theater room watching television. When he finally comes upstairs, I pretend to be fast asleep. He nudges me for sex, but I don't budge. He tries to pull me close to him, but I gently pull away. He gives up, and I hear him say [under his breath], "She must really be tired." Any other time, I would have never allowed Allen to leave me for days, and not make love to him, but I feel so horrible, so guilty ~ like I've betrayed him. Heck, I really don't know what I'm feeling right now. Tears are streaming down my face again, but I dare not let Allen see me. I can't bear to look him in the face, and lie any more than I already have. I finally fall asleep with a tear-stained pillow.

Its 5:30 a.m., and Allen jumps up, and prepares to head out to the airport. He wakes me before he leaves, gives me a big kiss, a tight squeeze, and says, "You owe me!" I knew exactly what he was talking about. I stretch and smile, "Owe you for what?" He says, "You'll find out when I get back." I just smile, and say, "Have a safe trip, Honey, and hurry back home to me." He says, "I miss you already," and gives me another big kiss, and leaves. I roll over, but I had a hard time going back to sleep. I feel terrible, but at the same time, I feel so good. I finally drift off to sleep, relieved that my new-found lover decides to let me rest.

Chapter Nine

I Know Who You Are . . .

WHEN I AWAKE, I quickly prepare to head out, as I'm on a mission; I need some answers. As I approach the door, I flinch when Mr. Invisible asks, "Where are you going? And, why are you ignoring me?" He's sure acting pretty darn familiar ~ like I belong to him. After last night, I'm no longer scared, but I am inquisitive. I respond, "Oh! You startled me, and for your information, I'm not ignoring you. I just have some errands to run." I scurry out of the house, and head straight for the library. I do need answers. Who is he? And, why is he in our house? I didn't want to go exploring from home, as I knew he'd distract me.

I'm at the library perusing through newspaper archives, searching to see if there was ever anything printed, connecting to our home address. I'm not sure what else to look for, but this is a start. I stumble across something in the Chicago Daily that catches my attention. "Bingo! Oh my God!" The article's heading reads: "Well-Know Architect, Addison Reid, Dies in Naperville Home ~ Body Found After 10 Days." His name was Addison Reid. They display his photo, along with 'our' address. Wow! He was absolutely gorgeous, with a hunk of a body. Is this who I've been making love to? Oh my! It was nice to be able to match a face and body, to the feelings. I move closer to the screen, and continue reading the rest of the article: "Multi-millionaire Architect, Addison Reid, was accidentally killed in his newly built mini-mansion on Page Court in Naperville while attempting to carry a 6 foot architectural design model down his winding staircase. Apparently, he lost footing and slipped. According to the coroner, Reid had been dead for nearly 10 days before his body was discovered." I gasp, "Oh, my God!" I continue reading: "The maid, Madalyne Polovski, had taken a two-week vacation to her native home of Poland." Mrs. Polovski's testimony: "When I looked through the glass doors, as I was putting my key in the lock, I noticed something big on the floor, but I just thought Mr. Reid dropped something, and forgot to pick it up. But, when I came inside, there was this horrible smell. I thought he had left some food out, and maybe it spoiled. As I walked closer to the staircase, I saw that it was him lying on the floor, in a puddle of blood, with this big thing lying on top of him, and part of it sticking out of him. It was horrible. The smell was horrible. I started screaming and called 911. I am so sorry that this happened to Mr. Reid. He was so nice to me and my family."

The article continues: "Reid was an only child, and both his parents were killed in a car accident two years earlier. His estate was..." My eyes are welling with tears, and I can't read anymore. This is so sad, and unbelievable. No wonder he can't leave his home. I feel so despondent. "I'm so sorry for you, Addison." I grab my purse, leave the library, and just sit numb in the car. What is wrong with me? How could I carry these feeling for someone I hadn't known ~ in this life? As I'm driving, I can't help but think about him. My head is engulfed with questions, "Did he die suddenly? Apparently, he wasn't married. Did he have a girlfriend?

Wouldn't she have missed him in 10 days? What about his friends? Oh, I'm so sorry for you, Addison."

Shoots, the phone rings and it's Ana. Urggg... I really don't feel like talking to her right now, but I have to because we're planning this party together. The only thing on my mind right now is Addison. I want to get to him. I need to touch him. I need to somehow reassure him... about what? I don't know. I answer the phone, "Hi Ana." She's her usual happy self, "Whatcha up to girl?" I reluctantly tell her about my excursion to the library, and what I discovered. There is silence on the other end of the phone. I can just imagine her facial expressions. She breathes heavily and then asks, "Why did you feel the need to research this? And, why did you need to go to the library to do so, when you have a quiet and peaceful office at home?" I reply, "Ana, it's kind of hard to explain, but things have been happening in the house again." There's another long silence on the other end of the phone. I speak up, "I know you don't believe me, but things have kind of turned in a different direction." She finally speaks, "Gayle, I thought you were pass all this? Did you go to see a doctor?" I respond, "No Ana! I did not go to see a doctor, and I don't need to go to see a doctor. Things are little different now, a little more intense than when I spoke with you about it before." She sarcastically blurts, "Can it get more intense than someone, who you can't even see, having sex with you?" I try to defend my cause, "You'll never believe it, Ana. Hell, I didn't even believe it, but now I know it's real." I pause and then confess, "He talks to me, Ana. Well, we talk to each other." There's another long pause on the other end, and then she says, "Okay Gayle! I'm not sure what you want me to say. I really want to be supportive, but this is a little too much for me. It's beyond comprehensive. I mean, I honestly can't believe that I'm hearing about this stuff again. I don't want to judge you, and I don't want to hurt your feelings, so let's just change the subject. Has Allen left yet?" I respond, "Yes, Ana. He left this morning. He'll be back in a few days." She asks, "Do you still want me to come up to help shop for the party?" I, unenthusiastically, say, "Yes. I really need your help." Honestly, I really didn't want her to come. In fact, I didn't even want to see her. I've got an attitude, and I'm very agitated, because she's not believing me. But, at the same time, I probably wouldn't believe her either. And besides, I need and want some time alone with Addison, and I don't need her interference right now. She says, "Gayle, I'll be there around 1:00ish, but I think it would be best if we didn't talk about him." I agreed, and we hung up. Ohhh… I regret that I ever said anything to her about Addison. I know she thinks I'm crazy, and I surely can't ever tell anyone else about this. Anyway, who would believe me? This will have to be my personal little secret (or should I say, "Big Secret")… from everybody.

I hurriedly drive back home. I want to touch him. I want to hear him. I want to love on him. I want to feel him inside me. I enter the house, and call out for him, "Hellooo, Where are you?" He answers, ever so softly, "I'm right here waiting for you." He grabs me around my waist from behind, and hugs me tight. I close my eyes, and take a deep breath. I

Love Never Dies!

can see his face in my mind, and feeling his touches, feel so good to me. I lean my head back on him, he kisses my neck, and caresses my breasts. He turns me to face him, and kisses me - his tongue deep in my mouth, so tantalizing, so comforting, and oh-so-good. He carries me to the family room, and lies me on the floor. He takes off my blouse, and removes my jeans. All I know is, I want him in me now. I beg him, "Please fuck me! Fuck me hard! Fuck me soft! Just fuck me." And that's just what he does. I just lie there in his arms, totally immersed, and in total bliss. I've never experienced anything or anyone like this. I wonder was he like this when he was alive? He's breathing heavily through his nostrils, and neither of us are saying anything. We're just feeling blissful.

After a while, I say, "I need to talk with you about something, and it's pretty important." He shifts his body towards me, as if to say, "You've got my undivided attention." He says, "Okay, I'm all ears. What's up?" As I was about to start confessing about what I found, the doorbell rings. "Oh Great! I completely forgot about Ana." I scurry, and put my clothes back on. "It's Ana; I'll have to tell you later. Darn it!" I jump up, and run to open the door. She's a bit apprehensive, and tries to be excited to see me. I could sense that she's a bit uncomfortable, so I try to pretend that everything is normal. "Heyyy girl... I'm glad you made it." Now, any other time, I'd be excited to see her, but this time, I wasn't so thrilled. I wish she would have made an excuse not to come. I wanted my time with Addison. As we're walking through the foyer, she gives me this odd look. I ask with a slight chuckle, "What's wrong with you?" She responds, "No, what's wrong with you? What's going on with that hair of yours?" I chuckle, "What's wrong with my hair?" She says, "Well, it's all smashed on one side, and kind of damp-looking on the other side." I say, "Okay! Okay! I took a little nap on the sofa." She says, "Huh, that I must've been some nap." We both laugh it off, and walk into the family room. Almost immediately, both our eyes catch sight of my panties lying on the floor. She walks over and picks them up with her car keys, in an icky kind of way. She says, "Ah, hello! Now what kind of nap did you say you were taking? Hum, that explains the hair." My shoulders drop, I smile, and give her this sheepish look. She giggles, "I know what you've been doing." I say, "You do?" She says, "Ahhh, yes!" I giggle, "I don't know what you're talking about, Ana," and I snatch my panties. She says, "I know you were in here getting off, Gayle ~ talking about you were taking a nap. Yeah right!" I smile and confess, "Busted!" We both fall on the sofa, and laugh. That sure broke the ice ~ a lot. I get up from the sofa, "Ana, help herself to a drink while I go upstairs and freshen up a bit." She looks over at me, smiles, and shakes her head, "Boy, you and your toys." I trot up the stairs, "Yep, can't imagine myself without them." She says, "Neither can I." We both burst out in laughter.

Chapter Ten

Ana's Annoyance . . . Go Home Ana!

I'M TAKING MY little bird bath, and Addison says, "Ohhh, she's pretty." I playfully reach out to smack him, "Don't even think about it! And, yes, she is pretty." He asks, "Have you told her about us?" I respond, "I tried to tell her, and now she thinks I need to see a shrink." Jokingly he asks, "Would you like me to make a believer out of..." I abruptly cut him off, "Ah, No! I don't want you to do anything! Besides, since no one believes me, this will be our forever secret ~ just you and me. He takes the wash cloth from me, and starts gently washing my vaginal area, as he's kissing my breast. I let out a nice, "Ahhh..." I pause, "Shhh, I hear something." It's Ana, right outside my bathroom door. "Darn it! What is she doing in my bedroom?" She shouts out, "Are you alright in there?" I answer, "Yesss! Why?" She replies, "Because I thought I heard you talking to someone." I tell her, "Don't be silly, Ana. Are you trying to make fun of me?" She says, "No, I'm not! It just sounded like you were talking to someone." I sarcastically say, "Whatever, Ana!"

I thought she'd walk away, but she's still standing outside my bathroom door. I remain silent, and then she speaks, "Um, I brought my overnight bag upstairs, and I wanted to know which room was mine." I respond, "Feel free to choose any room in this house, except this one." She laughs, and teasingly asks, "Why not this one?" We both chuckle. I open the bathroom door, and she is standing right in front of the door. Astonished, I ask, "Are you okay, Ana?" She's standing so close to the door that she has to step to the side, so I can come out. Then she answers, "Ah, yeah, I'm okay. I'm just looking around, and admiring this fabulous room of yours." She's such a bad liar. I know exactly what her nosey butt was doing. She was listening through the door. I didn't mention it though; I just played right along with her. She continues praising the house, "Gayle, this is what I call a master suite. Your description didn't give this house the justice it deserves. In fact, the entire house is just awesome. I could live like a queen in this place." I smile, "Thanks, Ana. I told you it was beautiful. You know, at times, I do feel like a queen, living in two worlds."

Addison audibly chuckles, as he gets it ~ he knows exactly what I'm saying. However, Ana is little baffled, as she jerks her head to and fro, trying to figure out where this sound is coming from. Then she asks, "What was that? Did you hear that?" I'm dying on the inside, because she's so clueless, and she's turned so pale. I grin and ask, "What was what?" She says, "Gayle, I heard something! I heard someone laughing." I give her this look, "Really, Ana! Now you sound like me!" She faint-heartedly laughs, "Oh boy, I retract that statement." We glance at each other, and give a slight snicker. I smile and ask, "Well, are you ready to shop?" She says, "Yes! Let's go!" We take the elevator to the main level, grab our purses, and head out through the garage door. As I'm exiting, Addison startles me, as he kisses me on my lips, and grabs my butt cheeks. I jump, and gasp. Ana quickly turns around, and gives me this perplexed look. I don't comment; I just keep walking, as if nothing happened. When she gets in my car, I look back, and smile at Addison. I purse my lips, throw him a kiss, and motion with my mouth, "You're such a naughty boy." I hear him faintly giggling. I get into the car with this big smile on face, and Ana, just looks over at me, but says nothing.

Ana is just talking and talking, and I'm just thinking and thinking… about You-Know-Who ~ Yep! ~ Addison. I'm thinking to myself, "He must not be able to leave the house, because I only hear and feel him when I'm home. Hum, an interesting observation and, I bet I'm right." We arrive at the store, grab two shopping carts, separate, and begin shopping for the party. A short while later, Ana shouts out, "Gayle, come here and check out these Party Plates. I'm only an aisle away, so I make my way over to her, and ask, "What are they? Oh, wait, here's a display sample. You place your drink in the center holder, and your food goes around the circumference of the plate." She excitedly says, "OMG! These will be perfect for the party. What do you think?" I hear her, but I don't hear her; I'm thinking about Addison. In a robotic tone, she says, "Gayle to earth… Gayle to earth… Do you hear me, Gayle?" I snap out of my little trance, "Of course I hear you, Ana, and you are right, these are awesome, and they need to be at every party. The ladies won't have to worry about someone putting anything vile in their drinks." She says, "Right! Let's get some!" I nod, "Okay, let's get some!"

We stopped at a few more stores, before dining at a nearby restaurant. There's a lot of small talk, but she dare not mention Addison. Heck, I dare not mention Addison. We wrap up, and head back home. I can't wait to get back to him; I know he's waiting for me. I feel like a little girl, with a schoolboy crush. What's gotten into me? Never mind! I know exactly what's gotten into me ~ Addison Reid!

As we're driving home, Ana comments, "Hey, you haven't talked to Allen all day." Oh Wow! She was right! How could I forget about Allen? I say, "Oh my goodness! Thanks Ana! We've been so busy that I totally forgot. I'll have to give him a call. But, he must be pretty busy, because he hasn't called me either." She's now probing, "It's funny, Gayle, I remember the last time he went out of town, you were calling him every other hour." I reply, "I know, Ana, but this time it's a little different, because you and I have been so preoccupied with the party and everything." I glance down at my phone, "Oh! Allen did call me; he called me twice. I didn't hear the phone ring, did you Ana?" She says, "No, I didn't. It was probably because of the poor reception in the stores." I say, "I'll call him back when we get back to the house." She looks over, and just stares at me like, 'really,' you're going to wait until you get home. I can see her staring at me, from my peripheral vision, but I completely ignore her. He's my husband, not hers.

Ana and I get back to the house, and after putting the groceries away, things are still a little awkward between us, so I decide that I'd better try to break the monotony. "Whew! I'm glad that's over, and I'm glad you're here with me, Ana." She responds, "I'm glad I'm here too, Gayle. That was fun, just like old times. I'm ready to relax now. What do you have to drink?" I say, "Well, I've got some pop, juice..." She cuts me off, "Ahhh, hello... something with a little more oomph, please." I laugh, "There's the bar! Help yourself, and pour me a glass while you're at it." As Ana is walking over to the bar, I discreetly look around for signs of Addison. I whisper, "Where are you?" I squeal, as he softly kisses me on my lips. I tap him, "You scared me!" Ana walks up on me with drinks in hand, "Here you go, Missy Lou." I say, "Thank you, ma'am." She asks, "Gayle, did you say something?" I respond, "Yeah, I said, "Thank you ma'am." She says, "No, I heard you say that, but before that I thought I heard you say something else." I tell her, "Well Ana, you probably heard me doing what I've always done since you've known me ~ talk to myself ~ or did you forget already?" She smiles, "Of course not, how could anyone who knows you forget that!" My mind is still on Addison; I want my time with him. I stretch, and yawn, "Ana, I'm a little exhausted. Do you mind if I go up and take a little nap." She says, "You know, that sounds like a good idea, and I think I'll do the same."

We go upstairs, and into our respective rooms. I close the door, and I'm smiling, because I know Addison is near. He wraps his arms around me from behind, and begins kissing my neck. I tell him, "You almost got me in trouble down there." He says, "I think you covered yourself very well. I missed you. I thought about you all day long, and I couldn't wait for my baby to come home to me." We frantically kiss each other, like we hadn't seen each other in a long time, and he unbuttons my blouse, to expose my ta-ta's. Unbeknownst to me, Ana opened my bedroom door, and peeked in.

She sees me being thrust onto the bed, and hears us giggling. She shouts, "Gayle!" I jump up, and close my blouse, "Ana, is everything okay?" She says, "I was about to ask you the same thing. What are you doing? What's going on in here?" I ask, "What do you mean, "What's going on in here? I'm getting ready for my nap, like we both said we were going to do! Why are you in here?" She says, "Well, I heard you talking, and laughing with somebody, and I wanted to see who?" I'm really trying not to get upset, but I'm pretty annoyed, "So, you just burst in my room without knocking?" She gives me this lame excuse, "Well, I wanted to be sure everything was okay. I know we're supposed to be the only ones in the house, but I heard voices." Annoyed, "What are you talking about, Ana? I was about to take a nap!" Then she has the nerve to snap, "I'm not crazy, Gayle! I heard voices, and not just your voice, but another voice also!" I say, "Don't be ridiculous, Ana; now you sound like me, again."

She's obviously agitated, but changes the subject, "Anyway, I also came to remind you to call Allen." I'm thinking to myself, "Why is she so concerned about me calling Allen?" But, I respond, "Oh, that's right! Thank you for reminding me, Ana." She says, "Remind you! Really Gayle!" I ignore her insinuation; and she actually stands there, waiting for me to call him. I pick up my phone, and dial Allen's number. He answers, "Hey Baby. I tried calling you twice today." I reply, "I'm sorry Honey, Ana and I were shopping and, apparently, my cell phone wasn't receiving any reception in the stores. I meant to call you back sooner, but afterwards, we went to eat, then got busy putting up the groceries, and girl-talking… you know how we are. Now, we're about to take a nap; we're a little exhausted, and do know that the wine didn't help any." We all give a little cackle, including Addison.

As Ana is looking around the room trying to find this other voice, she shouts out to Allen, "Hey Allen, how are you? I miss you." He says, "Hellooo Ana. I'm looking forward to seeing you, and your date next weekend." Ana shouts back, "Don't you worry about my date, Allen." We all laugh again, and I know Ana hears Addison's big mouth. Boy, he's really starting to unnerve me with this. He's going to ruin everything for us. Allen continues, "I'm trying to wrap things up quickly, so that I get back home to my baby." Ana cynically says, "Yeah, I think that's a good idea. You need to come home." I'm a little irritated, and want to get off the phone, so I say, "Okay Honey, hurry home. I love you. Bye-bye." Ana gives me this look of indignation. She wants to comment, but she just gets up to go to her room, "Well, Ms. Gayle, I'm going to try to take my nap now, and I think you should also." She leaves, and closes the door behind her. Addison remarks, "She's pretty intuitive isn't she?" I clarify, "What she is, is pretty nosey, but she knows me, Addison. We've been friends for a long time, and she's knows that something is off kilter." He responds, "Well, it's not like you didn't try to tell her, Gayle." I reply, "I know, Addison, but what I'm doing with you is not right. I mean, how much more of a dichotomy can this situation be – being in love with the living, and the dead? I'm all messed up. But you! What are you trying to do, get noticed or something? Why do you keep laughing and blurting out? People may not be able to see you, but they can sure hear you. Why are you doing this?" In a regretful tone, he says, "I'm sorry, Gayle. Sometimes I just forget, and get caught up in the moment." Sadly, I say, "I know it has to be difficult, but know that I'm here to make it a little easier for you." I lie down on the bed, and he nestles up next to me.

I'm tranquilly wrapped in his arms, but it must've just come to his remembrance that I actually called his name. He practically pushes me over, "Gayle, what did you call me? How did you know my name?" Cheerfully, I say, "Oh yeah! That's what I was trying to talk to you about earlier, before Ana arrived. I was curious about you, and this house, so I went to the library looking for answers, and I'm so happy that I found them." Well, he wasn't so optimistic. In fact, from his tone, he was a bit vexed, and bellows out a string of questions, "Why did you feel the need to do that? Why go to the library, when you have a computer, and all the technology you need right here at home? Why did you feel it necessary to dig up my past? It almost feels like you're snooping and/or invading my privacy." Defensively, I say, "Look, Addison! I wasn't trying to snoop or invade your privacy! I need to know who, and what I'm dealing with here! I mean, I move into this house, and encounter this unknown being, who I can hear and touch, but can't see ~ not to mention, who I end up sleeping with, and you don't think I need to know! And, for your information, the reason I went to the library is because I didn't want you distracting me. I kept asking you for answers, but you wouldn't divulge any, so I took it upon myself to do my own research." He exclaims, "Well, I hope you found what you were looking for!" I state, "Yes, I did! And, I have no regrets! The sad part, Addison, is, you could have just told me!" He softens his tone, "Gayle, I was going to tell you." Remembering that Ana is still in the other room, I quietly yell, "Yeah right! When?" He repentantly says, "You're right; I should have just told you everything. I guess I was just trying to wait for the right time. It's not easy, Gayle, and I've never had to explain it before. I'm sorry. Will you forgive me?" This was our first little tae-ta-tae, and I want it to be over, so I loosen the reigns, "Of course, I forgive you Addison. I don't want to argue with you. You've gone through enough. I know what happened to you, and I'm so sorry ~ so deeply sorry." He asks, "Now that you know, does it change anything?" I tell him, "Yes, it does. Now, I can visualize who I'm talking to, and who I making love with. I can even imagine your gestures." He chuckles, "Oh, you can gather all that from reading a newspaper article, and seeing my picture?" I answer, "Indeed! And, I'm truly sorry for you."

He gets sensitive, "I don't need your sympathy." I quickly respond, "And, you won't get any from me either. However, I do empathize, and I'm sorry for you." He asks, "Why are you sorry? It's not your fault." I respond, "I know, Addison, I'm just sorry about what happened to you; it seems so unfair."

He gets a little emotional, and I reach out for him. He comes close, and I embrace him. "Now I understand why you're here. You can't leave this house, can you?" He affirms, "No, I can't. For some reason, I'm bound here." I then ask the awkward question, "Is it okay for you to still be hanging around? I mean, you're…" He cuts me off, "I guess its okay. At least, nothing or no one has told me different." I then ask more awkward questions, "Did it happen instantly? I mean, did you know? Did you feel anything?" He readily answers, "Yes! Well, I assume it did. I wasn't in any pain. I just got up, and saw myself lying there in a puddle of blood. At first, I didn't realize what happened, but after a while, I figured it out. Initially, I was very resentful, because I felt that I had so much work to do here, like I wasn't finished living. I had no one. I had no wife, no parents, or any children. I didn't even have a will. It seemed so unfair. Everything just went to different organizations, trusts, and charities. I had no say so. I guess God had different plans for me. Either that, or I was just plain ole' clumsy, and left here before my time." I try to bring comfort to the conversation, "You know, Addison, none of us really know why God allows certain things to happen, but we do know that he's in total control, although some of the things we experience in this life can be pretty painful, and sometimes confusing. We still have to just trust Him." I can hear him sniffling, and I continue, "I don't know if this brings you any solace, but there was nothing but good things said about you ~ wonderful accolades from so many people." Soberly, he says, "You know, Gayle, I tried to help, and treat people right... you know, like I'd want to be treated." I compassionately respond, "Addison, you were, and are a really good person. I just wish I would have known you." He exclaims, "You are getting to know me now." Tears stream down my cheeks, and I let out a sigh, "I guess you're right." He kisses me on my forehead, and deliberately moves on to another topic.

When I saw you whisk through those entry doors, I said to myself, "Wow, she's beautiful." He continues, "I knew I wanted you. You were so happy, so vivacious, so captivating. I watched you sashay through every room. I was so happy that you were so happy, and pleased with my home." I'm blushing, "How could anyone not be pleased with this house? It's gorgeous. This house was the best surprise ever." He clears his throat, "Well, my beloved, I hear that you're planning a party." Delightfully, I respond, "Indeed, my love; indeed! I'm inviting my family and friends to see your beautiful home, and you'd better behave." He chuckles, "I will; I promise." He rolls me over on top of him, and unbuttons my blouse, again, and I quickly assist. I want to make him feel as good as he always makes me. I rub and caress his face and body, to feel where it begins and ends, and then I find my way back up to his penis ~ ummm... this lovely penis. He's already erect. I grab it in my hands, and begin to stroke it. He's moaning, and I gently maneuver his balls in my mouth, and begin to tickle them with my tongue. He's now moaning even louder. I consume his penis down the base of my throat, slurping and pulsating it with my tongue. I come up, mount, and ride this stallion. I pull out, and head back down, and begin glazing and gulping. He's gently pulling my hair, and moaning my name. I continue to suck him until he ejaculates. I'm waiting to ingest this gust of sperm, looking forward to it trickling down my lips, but there is none. It didn't matter, I knew he had cum, and I knew he was satisfied. I relax my head on his groin area, and he gently pulls me up into his arms. He says, "I love you, Gayle." I reply with assurance, "I love you back, Sir. Addison Reid." Oh my… what am I saying?

Addison and I are so wrapped up in each other that I totally forget that Ana is in the next room. Geez, I spoke too soon. She knocks, and then just abruptly opens my bedroom door, without waiting for me to answer, 'again.' She sees me lying naked, and then blurts out, "Gayle, what are you doing, and who's in here with you?" I sit up quickly, look over at her, and reach for my clothes to cover myself.

I shout at her, "Ana, what is wrong with you? Why do you keep thrusting yourself into my bedroom, without invitation? This is really becoming an annoyance!" Totally discounting what I said, she insistently asks, "What are you doing in here, and why are you naked?"

I want to throw her out, but I decide to stay civil, "I'm trying to rest, but you keep coming into my room, disturbing me. The room felt a little warm, so I took off my clothes and…" Then I catch myself, "Why do I need to explain this to you, Ana? What's up with you? Are you having a problem sleeping? What's the problem, Ana?" I'm a little perturbed and my tone says it. She responds, "Well, I was trying to sleep also, but I keep hearing voices, and …" I cut her off, "Voices! Again! Come on, Ana! I think you're the one paranoid. I'm trying to get a nap in!" She interrupts, "I know what I heard, Gayle." I say, "Perhaps you heard me talking to Allen again. I'm sorry if I woke you." She bellows out, "Gayle, this was no phone conversation that I heard." I bellow back at her, "Well, Ms. Know-It-All, what was it? I mean, you seem to know more than I do about what's happening in my bedroom? What exactly did it sound like, Ana?" Without hesitation, she says, "It sounded like two people having sex." I deeply sigh, "Really Ana! Two people having sex! Do you see two people?" She yells, "No, I don't Gayle, but I know what I heard." I say, "Like I said, you must've heard me on the phone with my husband, or maybe were you dreaming, and wishing you were having sex?" She gets upset, "No – I – wasn't – dreaming, Gayle! And, that was a really low blow." She then begins walking around my room, and looking in my closets. She sure has a lot of balls. I yell at her, "Ana, what the hell are you looking for?" She says, "It's not what, but it's who? I know you think I'm stupid, but I've been standing outside your door listening, and I know I heard you and another person ~ a man ~ talking, and making love, or should I say having sex? I even heard him calling your name." I patronize her, "Ana, I think you're the one who needs to see a doctor. Make the appointment, and I'll go with you." She's steaming now, "Don't patronize me, Gayle."

Ophelia Gayle

I want so badly to tell her to get the hell out of my house, but instead, I try to remedy the situation. "Ana, I'm trying to tell you that I was talking to Allen. I didn't get a chance to take care of him before he left, so I had to take care of him over the phone. I had the phone on speaker, so I could have free hands to 'work-it,' you know what I mean. I'm sorry if we disturbed you; that was not my intention. In fact, I totally forgot that you were here. You know how Allen and I are about our time. She's still suspicious, and not totally convinced, but says, "Well, why didn't you just say that? I'm sorry for jumping to the wrong conclusion. I should have just minded my own business, and stayed in my room." She starts out the door and turns back to me, "You little nasty thing you!" Relieved, I say, "Go to bed, Ana!" Addison and I quietly burst out in laughter. I knew she was still standing outside my door, as I could see her shadow under the bottom of the door, until she walked away. "Ha! I'm giving her a dose of her own medicine. When I was trying to tell her about you, she suggested that I see a doctor, so I'm just giving her the same advice. Ana's a long way from stupid though; she knows what she heard, but she can't prove what she heard." Addison is tickled pink, "Did you see the look on her face?" I fall back and laugh, "Yes, it was priceless. That made my day." We both lie quietly, until we fall asleep.

Gayle is fast asleep, and Addison decides to take a stroll down to Ana's bedroom. Ana is also (finally) asleep, with an empty wine bottle next to her. Addison pulls the hair back off her face, and softly kisses her. He whispers, "Hello Beautiful." Ana shifts her body a little, and goes back into a deep sleep. Addison begins rubbing her body, and tenderly sucking and caressing her breasts. Ana is breathing heavily, and moaning lightly. He takes succulent bites on her behind, and rubs her thighs. She slowly turns on her back, moaning and spreading her legs. As she stretches her arms, she feels the wine bottle next to her, picks it up and inserts the head of the bottle into her pussy. She's working that cunt, and she's working that bottle. Addison is now totally aroused, and takes full advantage of her drunkenness. He gently removes the bottle from her cunt, and begins sucking on her clit. She's so aroused that her body is quivering, and she is moving to his every beckon. He climbs on top of her, and slowly inserts his penis into her cunt. She arches her back, and lets out a loud moan, and begins fucking him frantically - like it's been a long time, and like she needs this dick. Suddenly, Ana opens her eyes wide, as if all drunkenness has abated. Her legs are spread open, and she's breathing heavily. She reaches and touches her vagina, and she's super wet, and slimy. She quickly sits up, but she's still too intoxicated to get up, falls back down on the bed, goes back to sleep. Addison is quietly laughing to himself, "That should knock her out for a while." He goes back to Gayle's bedroom, and cuddles up next to her, as she sleeps.

The next morning, I hear Ana fumbling around in the kitchen, so I put on my robe and go downstairs. She's sitting at the counter eating, and she's fully dressed. I'm feeling well rested and cheerful, "Good morning Lady Bug! Did you sleep well?" She turns and looks at me, "Good morning, Ms. Sunshine, I did end up finally getting a good night's sleep." She laughs out, "I think I had one of yours dreams, except I woke up only to find that I had been fucking the wine bottle that I emptied last night." We both crack up. I say, "Ana, you're a fool." She agrees, "I know it, girl, but too bad it couldn't have been the real thing. You know how long it's been?" I reassure her, "Don't worry, Ana, Mr. Right is coming soon, and he's going to tear that pussy up!" We both crack up. Then out of the clear blue, she asks, "Hey, what was the architect's name who lived in this house." I answer, "Addison Reid. Why?" She has this mysterious look on her face. I ask again, "Why?" She says, "No reason in particular. I just thought about him ~ poor guy. You never know your tomorrows, do you?" I say, "Nope! You really don't. That's why it's important to live a happy and fulfilling life for as long as you can." She then somberly says, "Gayle, I heard you say his name last night." Exasperated, I say, "Ana, I know we're not going to go through this again; it's too early. I told you that I was on the phone with Allen." She skeptically says, "Okay, you were on the phone with Allen!" I notice her baggage at the front door, and I ask, "Are you leaving this early?" She says, "Yes! I need to get back to Milwaukee; I've got tons of work to do." She's not supposed to leave until later this afternoon. Hum, I wonder why she's leaving so early, but I don't care; I want her to go home. She then asks, "Gayle, what time will Allen be home?" I answer, "He'll be home later this evening. Why?" She's probing again, "Well, I just find it odd that you've barely mentioned his name since I've been here." I breathe deeply, "What are you talking about, Ana? I've talked to Allen a couple times since you've been here. What are you digging for?" She says, "Look! I don't want to argue with you about your business, Gayle, so I think I'm going to make my way back home." I respond, "That's probably best, as I don't want to argue with you either, especially about 'my' business." She walks to the door, picks up her bags, and turns toward me, "I'll see you at the party." I walk over, and open the door. "Thanks for coming, and for helping, Ana." She nods, gives me smirk, and walks out the door. Normally, I would have walked her to her car, but I was actually glad to see her leave. I was pretty fed up with her, as she had become a real nuisance.

And besides, I want to spend more time with Addison, before Allen returns from his business trip.

Whew! I close the door and walk back into the room. I tell Addison, "I don't like the way we left things. She's my very best friend, and while she doesn't understand what's going on, I do." He reiterates, "Well, it's not like you didn't try to tell her, and if she would have listened and/or believed you, I could have confirmed what you told her, and she wouldn't have spent the night fucking a wine bottle." We both laugh out loud. No more worries about who can hear us. I tell him, "Thank you very much for behaving yourself while she was here."

Chapter Eleven

You, Me, and He . . . Shear Ecstasy

ADDISON AND I are sitting on the sofa, and he asks, "How long have you and Allen been married?" I respond, "Allen and I have been married for three and a half years. What about your relationships, Addison?" He says, "Well, I've never been married, but I was once engaged. I wanted her to move here with me, but she declined. She argued that I put my work ahead of her, although I really wasn't trying to. She just couldn't understand that everything I was doing was for us – for our future, but she wasn't buying it, and she left me. She mailed her engagement ring back to me in an envelope." Appalled, I say, "Wow! That sure made it final. I'm so sorry." He chuckles, "You're so sweet. Why are you always so sorry for things that you had nothing to do with?" I say, "Well, I guess I'm just sorry about the unfortunate outcomes."

I confess, "I never in million years thought that I'd ever cheat on Allen. He's my life, Addison. How could I do this to him? Since you and I have been together, I hardly ever think of Allen. A part of me feels so guilty. I love him, but I also love you. I think about you every awakening moment. I can't even write, because I'm thinking of you. I rush home, because I can't stand being away of you. I'm so confused. My life with Allen was perfect before we moved here. I love him, but I don't want to give you up. I don't know what to do, Addison. How can I look at Allen the same? I'm in love with another man. I'm living this big lie." Addison tries to soothe me, "Well, do you consider what we have a 'relationship,' being that I'm deceased?" I shrug, "Yeah, that's the logic that I'm trying to use, but, Addison, you're tangible. I can feel you. I can touch you and, hell, I'm even making love to you - every chance I get, and it's the best love-making that I've ever had, outside of Allen. Wouldn't you consider that a relationship? In my twisted little mind, I'm in a relationship with you, and I don't ever want it to end. It's like a fairy tale. But Addison, you've got to promise that you'll help me keep this secret between the two of us. If Allen ever finds out, he'll never forgive me." Addison draws me close to him, "I assure you that this will be our secret forever, as I don't want to lose you either, Gayle." I feel a warm calm, as I lie in his arms.

Addison says, "You know, Gayle, I never believed in love at first sight until I saw you. It was something about you that just took my breath away. I just wanted to eat you up the moment you came walking through those doors. I didn't think I'd ever get this chance again. I guess that's why I'm so adamant about making you feel special." I smile, and tilt my head up to find his lips. I get up and say, "I do feel so special, but I must get back to reality. I need to run out, and get dinner for Allen." He spurts out, "What! Really!" I giggle, "Yes, Addison, Really! I'm still a wife, and he's still on his way home." I get showered, dressed, and make my way to the grocery store. I hate to leave him, but I have to always remember that Allen is my first priority, even though it doesn't appear that way.

I return home, and hurriedly start preparing dinner for Allen and me. Addison and I are talking and laughing, while I'm cooking. How I enjoy our conversations. Allen and I used to talk like this all the time. I finally finish cooking. "Addison, I really need to try to get some work done." Drudgingly, he says, "I understand; I won't bother you, Gayle." A couple hours later, I hear the garage door opening. I shout out, "Addison." He answers, "I'm right here, darling." My voice is stern, "Addison, Allen is home; please, please behave." He kisses me, "I promise. I promise." I head over to the garage door to greet my husband. Allen comes in and shouts out for me, "Honey, I'm home! Mmm… Something smells so good." I greet him with a big, juicy kiss. He picks me up, swings me around, and says, "Oh, how I've missed you." Happily, I say, "I've missed you too, handsome, and I'm glad you're home." Honestly, I don't know if I'm so glad that he's home. I've been enjoying my time with Addison. Allen gives me a big hug and squeeze, and says, "I don't like being away from you." I look up at him and smile, "Dinner is ready, Baby." He's so happy that he yells out, "Woo-hooo, you made dinner ~ for little ole' me! Why, thank you ma'am. Let me run up, and freshen up a bit, and I'll be back in a jiffy."

Addison comments, "Urggg…That was really hard to watch." I ask, "What was hard to watch, Addison?" He responds, "Allen kissing you like that!" I wave my hand at him, "Don't be silly Addison; that's my husband. Do I detect a bit of jealousy?" He replies, "Ah… Maybe!" Now, I'm a little annoyed, "What's wrong with you, Addison? It's not like you don't know that I have a husband." He says, "Oh yeah! I do know that you have a husband, but you said that you loved me, Gayle, but when he's around, you ignore me." I retort, "I do love you, Addison, but that doesn't negate the fact that I have a husband, who

I just happen to love as well, and who happens to still be alive and well." Realizing what I just said, I begin to apologize profusely, "I'm so sorry; I shouldn't have said that to you, Addison. It didn't come out right." The room was silent, and I knew I hurt his feelings. He speaks in a glum tone, "I understand your position, Gayle." I say, "Addison, please don't be like that. Can we talk about this tomorrow? I need to give Allen 'his' time now. We had a good time while he was away, didn't we? Didn't I give you all of me?" He answers, "Yes, you did, Gayle." I ask, "Then, please give me this time with my husband. Please?" He agrees, "I will, I promise, and I do understand, even though I don't like sharing you with him." I'm thinking to myself, "It's really the other way around; he's sharing me with you."

Allen comes back into the kitchen, "Hey Babe, "Who were you talking to?" I chuckle, "I wasn't talking to anyone; I was singing." He sarcastically says, "Oh boy, I forgot about your singing, or should I say your 'not-so' singing." We both start laughing, because everyone knows that I can't sing. He says, "I'm hungry, let's eat." We enjoy our meal, and he gets up to help me clean the kitchen. We're teasing and playing around, when suddenly we hear a glass drop to the floor and break. He says, "Uh Ohhh… I must've accidently tapped when I swung the towel at you." I knew better, and I look around the room, giving Addison the evil eye. Allen cleans up the broken glass, and we resume cleaning the kitchen.

Allen begins caressing my ass, and pulling me close to him, so that I can feel his erection. We give each other that look like - I know what you want. I run toward the stairs, and he runs behind me - we're laughing hysterically. We get to the bedroom, and start ripping each other's clothes off. We didn't waste any time getting down to business.

I was wet and juicy, and he was as hard as a brick. I owed him, so I wanted to give him a little something special. I roll him over, spread his legs, and bury my head between them. I begin sucking his dick, and fondling and licking his nuts. Allen is moaning ever so loudly, and I'm getting off just hearing him. I'm on my knees, working my clit with one hand, and stroking his rod with the other. Suddenly I gasp, because I feel Addison's big, slippery cock entering my pussy, and his thumb working my asshole. I'm completely over the top, and can hardly concentrate on sucking Allen's dick, because I'm so focused on what's happening to 'my' body from behind. "Lord, help me!" Addison glides his dick out of my pussy, and gently slides it into my rectum. "Ahhh... Goodness-gracious!" He's smoothly stroking, and I'm in total bliss, about to lose my natural mind. Allen is breathing heavily, about to reach his climax, and I'm a second away from exploding into ecstasy. Addison is also about to cum, as his strokes are moving faster and his cock is getting harder. I'm saying to myself, "Lord, please don't let Addison cry out." Allen lets out this long holler, as his cum is spurting in my mouth, and onto my face. Then, Addison and I together squeal out right behind him. Between Allen's heavy breathing, and our screeching, you couldn't tell who's who or what's what. Thank goodness! The three of us collapse in sheer contentment.

I lie at Allen's side, and Addison's body is cropped at my backside. I'm feeling too good to have an attitude with Addison right now. Normally, Allen would rest a moment, and start back up again, but I was praying that he'd fall asleep, because Addison had already done a nice job working my cunt, and my ass; and, I was totally satisfied. Allen quickly falls asleep, and Addison is caressing and kissing my body. I turn over to face him, and he thrusts his tongue in my mouth, and gives me a long, passionate kiss. He whispers, "Thank you, my love." I respond, "Thank you." We fall asleep ~ you, me, and he...

Early the next morning, Allen rolls over, and begins kissing and groping. He wants to finish what he started last night. I, on the other hand, was not ready for another round just yet, but he was so insistent. He says, "Honey, I'm sorry I fell asleep on you last night. I didn't mean to short-change you; I was just so tired from travelling." I reply, "You don't have to explain, Allen. I was elated just watching you get off. Besides, I owed you, remember?" He's still being a little frisky, "Yeah, but I need to feel me inside you." I ask, "Allen, can we wait, and start up a little later; I'm still getting my beauty sleep." He says, "You just lie there, and I'll do the rest." Oh boy! He climbs on top, and begins making love to me, telling me how much he enjoyed the blow-job I gave him last night. I'm feeling a little (and I mean, a little) guilty. All of a sudden in the middle of his stroking, he cascades off of me, and onto the floor. I abruptly jump up, "What happened?" [Like I didn't know]. He says, "I'm not sure, Gayle, but it felt like someone just pushed me over." He starts laughing, so I start laughing with him. I'm flabbergasted, "Oh my goodness! Babe, you scared me! Are you okay?" He giggles a little, "Yeah, I'm fine, but that was weird." He climbs back up on me, inserts himself, and continues stroking his pussy. He flips me over, and starts loving me from the back. Oh wee… He feels so good. He's gently slapping my ass and stroking fast, and then collapses with relief. He lies there for a moment, and pulls me close to him. After a while, he gets up, and goes into the bathroom.

When Allen goes into the bathroom, I get up, grab my robe, and run downstairs. I'm walking around looking for any signs of Addison. I whisper, "Addison! Addison Reid, where are you?" Addison doesn't answer. He knows that I'm pissed. I continue calling out for him, "Addison! I know you hear me calling you!" He's still not answering, and as I turn around, Allen is standing right in front of me. I nearly jump out of my skin. He asks, "What are you looking for, Gayle, and who is Addison? I look at him, and ask with indignation, "What are you talking about, Allen?" He lashes back, "What do you mean, what am I talking about, Gayle? I come out of the bathroom to ask you a question, and you were gone, so I come downstairs looking for you, and when I get to the bottom of the stairs, I hear you walking around, calling out for someone named 'Addison.' Who is Addison?" I try to play it off, but I don't know if it's working. "Allen, I was trying to remember where I put my medicine, so what you kept hearing me say was, Medicine... Medicine... Where is my medicine?" He gives me this 'I'm not stupid' look, "What medicine, Gayle?" I respond, "You know, the medicine for my migraine headaches." He asks, "When did you get a headache? You didn't tell me you had a headache. And, since when do you take medicine for migraines?" Agitated, "Never mind, Allen. Why don't you go run the Jacuzzi; I'll be up in a minute. I want to look in one more place." He sighs, "Okaaay, but you've been acting a bit strange lately." Whew! That was too close for comfort. What is Addison trying to prove? He promised me that he'd behave. I'm so mad at him right now, that I could spit.

I climb into the Jacuzzi with Allen, and he asks, "Did you find your medicine?" I respond, "No, but it's okay; the Jacuzzi should do the trick." He just looks over at me, but doesn't say a word. We're just relaxing, and enjoying our morning. I'm in his arms, and we're softly chatting. Suddenly, the jets cut off. OMG! I sit up, roll my eyes, and turn the jets back on. Allen, of course, has no clue what's going on, but I'm fully aware of what's happening. He says, "Honey, I should be able to start spending more time with you. My workload will be getting a little lighter, because of the new hires and, I'm nearly finished with a big case that I've been working on." A bitter-sweet sensation comes over me, "That sounds good to me, Allen." What am I to do with Addison, if Allen is home more often? He's already misbehaving. What is Addison trying to do, sabotage, and ruin my marriage? I'm so pissed at him right now. We lie back, close our eyes, and just relax, but I can't rest now, because I know that Addison is lurking close. How dare him! He's had all my time for the last few days, and even stole some of Allen's time last night, now he wants to act like this. I'm appalled, and disappointed.

I'm still looking around, giving Addison the evil eye. I know he sees that I'm mad. After about 15 minutes, the jets automatically turn off, and we get out of the Jacuzzi and begin drying ourselves. Allen is watching every curve of my body, and then decides that I need a little help drying myself. He's such an animal. He's now on his knees tonguing away on my clit. I collapse over his shoulder, as I come to a climax while standing up. That's the craziest feeling; you get so weak at the knees that your legs just buckle under you. Ummm, it feels so good. Addison slaps me on the behind, while I'm bent over across Allen's shoulders. Allen straightens me up and says, "What was that?" I say, "You tapped my butt." He says, "No, I did not tap your butt." I say, "Then who did?" He stands up, and looks at me, "I don't know, Gayle, but it wasn't me?" I look at him like, "Why are you looking at me?" Then he says with a stern face, "Hum… I'm not sure what that was." I look at him, hunch my shoulders and say, "Me either," and, I walk away. Things are quiet, as we're getting dressed. I don't want to go downstairs by myself, so I wait until Allen is dressed, and we take the elevator down to the main level.

Chapter Twelve

The Housewarming Close Encounters

IT'S SATURDAY, AND it's the day of our Housewarming party. Allen and I are in the kitchen, excitedly planning our morning. We resolve that we're going out for a quick breakfast, he's dropping me off at the salon, and he's picking up the liquor, and other miscellaneous items for the party. As Allen and I are leaving, Addison grabs my arm, but I'm so furious with him that I just give a stern look, jerk away, and continue walking out to the car. Everything went according to our plans, and we make our way back to the house. We've got about 3 ½ hours before the guests arrive, so we hurriedly unpack everything, and start the preparations. Allen turns on some upbeat music, and we're dancing and singing, while setting things up.

I'm thinking, "Good! No signs of Addison." Uh oh... I speak too soon. He touches my arm. I look down at my arm, pull away, but I don't acknowledge him. He touches me again, but I just ignore his touches. When Allen goes out on the Terrace to start decorating, Addison possessively says, "I haven't seen you all day, Gayle! Why are you deliberately ignoring me?" I shout in a whisper, "Of course you haven't seen me; I've been gone all day! And, yes! I am ignoring you! I'm super-pissed at you for that stunt that you pulled last night! How dare you!" He's defensive, "You've been ignoring me ever since Allen came home!" I lash out, "Look! You know how I feel about you, and you also know that I can't just drop everything to give you my undivided attention! I have a husband, Addison!" He says, "I know that, but I miss us, Gayle. I've gotten so used to you being with me, and it's hard not being able to communicate with you." I beg him, "Addison, please just let me get through this night. It'll be alright; I promise." He kisses me on my lips. I push at him, and say in a demanding tone, "Stop it, Addison!" He then strikes out, "Perhaps we need to do something about Mr. Allen." Defensively, I ask, "What do you mean, "Do something about Mr. Allen?" He hears my tone, and says, "Oh, nothing."

I express my frustration with him, "Addison, I am so disappointed in your behavior. You promised me that you wouldn't act up, but that's all you've been doing since Allen walked through the door. You're making this really hard for me." He apologizes, "I'm sorry, Gayle." I respond, "Yeah, that's what you keep saying, but I can't tell by your actions." He says, "I guess I'm just feeling a little jealous, and left out." I tell him, "Well, you're going to have to get over it now, and wait until tomorrow." Oh, no! Allen is standing in the doorway, "Honey, who are you talking to?" I look over at him and smile, "I was singing, Honey." He says, "No Gayle, you weren't singing this time; you were talking." I confess, "You know, Allen, I probably was. I'm trying to make sure I have everything in order for the party so, I may have, very well, been talking." He just looks at me, and leaves the room. I whisper, "I don't know how I'm going to keep this going. Addison, you're making it very difficult for me, and you're really starting to stress me out."

Addison whispers in my ear, "Meet me in the powder room." I bellow out, "Are you crazy? You know I can't meet with you right now; I've got company coming, and lots to do before they get here!" He pleads with me, "Please, Gayle." I shake my head, "Addison, why are you doing this now? You have no need to feel insecure. I do love you, and when this is over, I promise, you can have all of me." He pleads more, "Prove that you love me, Gayle, and come into the powder room with me." Knowing that he's not going to let up, I, annoyingly, let out a heavy sigh, and storm into the powder room. He's right behind me, bumping and caressing my ass. I can feel his erected penis bouncing off my ass as I walk. He closes and locks the door, and wastes no time getting busy. I thought I was a nymph, but he takes the case. He swiftly pulls my panties down, props me on the edge of the sink, quickly penetrates my vagina, and he's thumping baby. I let out a loud moan, as I come to a climax, "Ohhh, Addison, you know you drive me crazy." This man is so damn irresistible, and so damn horny. He lets out an unnecessarily loud grunt, as he's busting his nuts. He embraces me and softly says, "Thank you." He grabs a hand towel, soaps it up with warm water, and gives me a gentle wash-down. Boastfully, he says, "Now tell me you don't miss this." I smile, "Yes, I do; now let me get back to work."

Allen knocks on the bathroom door, and asks, "Honey, are you okay in there?" Startled, I answer, "Yes, I'm fine! Can't a girl have some privacy?" I flush the toilet, turn on the water, as if I'm washing my hands, and open the door. He's standing right in front of the door, with this dubious look on his face. He walks pass me, and into the powder room. He's suspiciously looking around, "Gayle, what's going on?" I ask, "What are you talking about now, Allen?" He picks up the wet towel, looks at me, and asks, "Were you masturbating?" I feel a sense of relief, because I thought he was going to say that he heard me talking to someone again. I'm thankful that he didn't, so I lie and say, "Okay, I confess, I was having a moment, and needed a quick release." He asks, "Why didn't you just call me? You know I have no problem taking care of my girl." He unzips his pants, and starts unbuckling his belt. I quickly zip his pants back up, and tell him, "No! No! No! That will have to wait until later." I quickly walk back into the kitchen. Allen walks away, and says, "Okaaay, but you don't know what you're missing." I'm thinking to myself, "Absolutely nothing." I'm totally satiated after making love to Addison. Addison whispers, "I won't bother you again tonight." I smile, "Thank you!"

Allen comes back in about 30 minutes later, "Alrighty, I'm done with everything out on the Terrace. Do you need me to help you with anything inside?" I respond, "Nope! I'm done also; let's get dressed." We look at the clock, and we've got about 40 minutes. We eyeball each other, and race up the stairs ~ laughing hysterically.

My relationship with these two men seem almost normal. I never thought I'd see the day when I'd long for anyone, but Allen. I often think of this song from back in the day, "Trying to Love Two, Ain't Easy to Do..." But it is easy when one is a ghost. In fact, I'm enjoying this more than ever. However, my challenge is the schedule. I need to appropriately figure out how to schedule my intimate time between the two of them. I certainly can't talk with Allen about this, but I will have a talk with Addison about it. We can work something out where everyone is happy. Yeah, that's it; I'll talk about it with Addison tomorrow. He's the one who seems to have an issue with my time. His problem is, he doesn't want to share me, and that's not a good.

The doorbell rings, and Allen goes downstairs to welcome the guests. I hear all the commotion; it's so exciting. I chuckle, and continue applying the finishing touches to my makeup. I can hear the loud greetings, much laughter, and lots of "Ohhh's and Ahhh's." Allen comes back upstairs and says, "Honey, are you near ready? Lots of people are starting to gather, and even more are coming." I say, "Yes! I'm ready." We take the elevator down, and as the doors open, I'm surprised to see that so many of our guests have already arrived. I begin greeting everyone with hugs and kisses, and thanking them all for coming, as more are still coming through the door. The house is filled with joy and laughter. Allen turns on some soft music, and everyone is having a grand ole' time. Everyone is asking for a tour, as they are in awe of the house. Allen shouts out, "Follow me for the grand tour!" Everyone starts laughing, and eagerly follows Allen. I stand back smiling, and waving, "I'll see ya'll when ya'll get back!" They all chuckle, and commence on the tour.

I excitedly retreat into the kitchen, and call out for Addison. He responds, "I'm right here, Love." I proudly tell him, "It's all about your house. Everybody wants to see your house, Addison." He says, "Yes, it is kind of exciting, Gayle. I never got the chance to show it off." I tell him, "Well, you're doing it vicariously through me now." He agrees, and says, "I love you so much, Gayle." He's standing behind me, just holding me close, as I lie my head, contently, on his shoulder. I turn around to kiss him, and I'm alarmed to see Ana just standing there with her hand covering her mouth, in astonishment. "Oh my God!" was all she could say.

I walk toward her, and she clams up. I ask, "Are you okay, Ana? What's wrong?" She looks horrified, but shrugs her shoulders and says, "Nothing! Nothing's wrong!" And, she hurriedly walks away. I have a distinct feeling that she heard Addison and me talking. I mean, she was just several feet away. I chuckle to myself, "Let's see who needs a doctor now!"

The crowd's coming back around, everyone is mingling, and having a great time. I make the announcement, "Everyone, please feel free to start eating. Everything is buffet style, so grab a Party Plate, a drink, and eat up." Everyone is commenting on The Party Plates, and how convenient they are. I just led them to the website, *www.thepartyplate.com*, and told them to peruse through the site, at their leisure. I'm just glad that they were a success.

Ophelia Gayle

Addison makes me jump, as he whispers in my ear, "What a successful party, my dear." Between my teeth, and as I'm smiling, I ask him, "What are you doing here? You promised to behave." He responds, "Where else am I supposed to go? I'm not doing anything. I'm just looking." All the while, Ana is practically staring down my throat. I know she sees my lips moving, as I'm trying really hard to be discreet. Addison rubs my thigh, and my dress rises on one side. I slap his hand, and tell him, "Stop!" I look over at Ms. Nosey, and she's looking flabbergasted, and quite pale. I walk over to her, and ask, "Are you enjoying the party, Ana?" She says, "Yes!" There such a distance between us, so I stand next to her, just to make small-talk. She folds her arms, gives me this half-hearted smile, and asks, "Are you enjoying your party, Gayle?" Excitedly, I tell her, "Yes! I'm having the best time ever." Sarcastically, she says, "I just bet you are." I ask, "Now, what's that supposed to mean, Ana?" She says, "I'll talk to you about it another time ~ after the party. I think we really 'do' need to talk." I tell her, "Okay! But try not to be so intense. It's a party, lighten up, and have some fun." She walks away from me. I know she's more than suspicious now, and she wants some answers, but I won't have any for her. How about that!

Well everyone is leaving, and Allen and I are escorting the last of our guests out the door. We close the door, and slide down to the floor. We look at each other, sigh, and smile. I lean my head on his shoulder, "Whew! What a party! I had so much fun." He says, "Me too! It's 2 a.m. Let's lock up, and go to bed." I tell him, "You go on up, Honey; I need to clean up this mess." He grabs my arm, "Oh, no you're not! We'll deal with that tomorrow. I know how you are, but you'll survive not cleaning up for one night." I give in, "Okay, okay, you're right. I'm tired too." We both go upstairs, and I look and listen ~ No sign of Addison. Thank God!

Chapter Thirteen

All Hell Breaks Loose

WE WAKE UP the next morning, still a little tired from last night. Stretching, I ask, "What time is it?" Allen responds, "Who cares? We have nowhere to go, and nothing to do. It's our day." He dives under the blankets, and starts playfully caressing and tickling me. I'm laughing and telling him to stop. We're just enjoying each other, when out of nowhere, Addison decides to loudly clear his throat. Allen stops frolicking and asks, "What the hell was that?" I ignorantly ask, "What was what?" He says, "I heard something. It almost sounded like someone clearing their throat." I play it off, "I didn't hear anything, but please don't tell me that 'somebody' didn't leave the party last night?" He says, "Well, I'm going down to see. It might've been one of my crazy cousins; you know how they are." Allen gets up, grabs his robe, and rushes downstairs.

I call out, "Addison! What are you doing? What's wrong with you? You promised me…" Addison cuts me off, "Promised you what ~ that I'd be a good ole' boy. Well, I am being good, but I just want to remind you that I'm still here, and you're talking about staying in bed with him all day." I shout in a whisper, "I did not say that I was staying in bed all day! All I ask is for you to let me get pass the party, and I will make time for us." He doesn't say anything. I continue, "Allen will be off to work in the morning, and then it's just you and me, Baby. He says, "I know, I know. I just miss the hell out of you, and, I hate to see you lying with him." I try to pacify him, "I miss you also, Addison, but it's not like I've completely ignored you. You did get a 'quickie' right before the party, didn't you?" He sighs, "Yeah, I know, and it was absolutely delicious." I say, "Okay then! Stop complaining, and stop acting like you don't know that I have a husband." He says, "How can I forget, Gayle? You're flaunting him in my face." I tease, "Awww... My baby's a little jealous. Come here, big daddy, and give mama some sugar." He asks, "Why are you trying to tease me?" I respond, "I'm just giving you a taste of what it will be once we're alone, just you and me."

Unbeknownst to me, Allen had come back upstairs, and he overheard the conversation between Addison and me.

He comes back into the bedroom, and I jokingly ask, "Hey Babe, did you find any leftover guests?" He responds in a very 'nasty' tone, "No, but who the hell are you talking to?" I reply, defensively, "Here we go again! What are you talking about, Allen? I'm not talking to anyone!" He blurts out, "Really Gayle! Do you think I'm really that stupid? I heard him talking, and I heard you talking about this 'quickie' that you gave him before the party?" He starts, furiously, searching around the room, and into the closets, "Where the hell is he, Gayle? If I find him, I'm going to kill him!" O.M.G.! I know I'm busted, but I don't know what else to say, so I ask again, "What are you talking about, Allen?" He's enraged, and he steps over to me, points his finger in my face, and grinds his teeth, "Whatever you do, don't you dare try to patronize me!" I'm scared to death, because I've never seen him behave like this. He continues, "I stood outside that bedroom door, and listened to your conversation with God knows who!" He's fuming, tossing furniture, and looking everywhere, even out the window. He asks again, "Where is he?" I just stand there crying, because I know that I'm in big trouble. He says, "You've been sooo distracted lately, and I've been sooo fucking stupid, believing that you're walking around talking to yourself. You'd better start talking, and I mean now!" I can't stop crying. I look at him, and shake my head, "Allen, I really don't know what to say!" I get up to go to the bathroom, he grabs my arm, and insists, "You'd better tell me something!" I scream out, "Allen, let me go! You're hurting my arm!" He says, "Gayle, I'm not letting you go until you explain to me what the hell is going on!" I holler at him, "Let go of my arm, Allen!" And, out of nowhere, Addison shouts, "You heard the lady; let her go!" Allen releases my arm, and he's looking around, trying to find the person with the voice. He picks up a lamp, looking around mysteriously, "Where the hell are you? Come on out, and face me like a man!" I speak up, "You can't see him, Allen?" Confused, he says, "What! What do you mean, I can't see him?" Addison blurts out, "You might as well tell him, Honey." Allen shouts, "Honey! What! Who the..." Allen is so bamboozled that he's walking in circles, "Gayle, you wanna tell me what the fuck is going on!" Addison prompts, "Tell him, Gayle." I yell, "Addison, please!" Allen is so baffled, "Yeah, Gayle, tell me... Wait a minute... what am I hearing? Who am I hearing?" Addison just won't stop egging things on. I'm sobbing hysterically, and as I sit on the bed, I slowly begin to speak. I'm stuttering, and I'm scared, "Allen, I don't know where to start." He yells at me, "Try from the fucking beginning, Gayle!" I'm so embarrassed that I can't look him in the face. "I'm so ashamed, Allen, and I don't know how to tell you." Addison provokes the situation even more, "Oh, just tell him, Gayle! Just fucking tell him!" I shout, "Addison, please shut the hell up." I'm breathing deeply, but manage to get out, "I've... I've been kind of... involved with someone." Allen shouts, "What the hell is kind of involved? Either you are or you aren't involved! It's like, you can't be kind of pregnant – either you are or you aren't!" I try to get the words out, "Allen, it's hard to explain." I'm sobbing, snorting, and tears are in rare form, covering my entire face. "I think I'm having an affair." He says, "Gayle, you're not making any damn sense! Are you or aren't you having an affair?" I respond, "I don't know if it's really an affair, but I've been sleeping with someone."

Allen is in total shock. He drops the lamp, falls to his knees, and he's crying hysterically. He buries his face in his hands, crying and shouts, "You've got to be fucking kidding me! How could you, Gayle? How could you do this to me? How could you do this to us? Why? What happened?" I respond, "Allen, I tried to tell you, but..." Allen interrupts, "Tell me what?" Addison speaks out, "If you really want to know, then stop interrupting, and give her a chance to explain." Allen gets up angrily, "You mother... You really need to stay out of this! And stop trying to tell me how to deal with 'my' wife. Wait... wait... Who the fuck are you? What the fuck are you?" With indignation, Addison says, "My name is Addison, and she's been trying to tell you about me, but you were so busy patronizing her..." I cut him off, "Addison, please shut up!" I continue, "His name Addison Reid. He was the Architect who designed this house; he was accidentally killed..." Allen cuts me off, "What the hell does that have to do with anything?" Addison interrupts, "If you weren't so rude, she could finish telling you the whole story." Allen shouts, "I'm warning you, buddy! This is between me and my wife." Addison sarcastically says, "And me!" I yell, "Addison, please, please shut the fuck up!"

Allen is obviously furious and befuddled, "Wait a minute; I heard you calling out that name, Addison, and you swore that you were looking for your 'medicine'. You're such a liar!" Allen is crying, and shaking his head profusely. He's pacing in front of me, "Go ahead, Gayle, finish! Let me hear you try and explain this shit to me." I continue, "Well, do you remember when we first moved in, and I told you I heard something." He doesn't respond. I pause, "Well, that was Addison. I didn't know it then, but as time passed, and more things started happening, I realized that there was someone else living in the house, besides us." Allen's eyes grow wider, and he just looks at me. I resume, "Addison is a ghost - a ghost who hasn't crossed over, and is bound to this house." Allen shouts, "Gayle, this is some straight up bullshit. What you're saying doesn't make any sense." I say, "I know, Allen, it was hard for me to believe, at first. And then, I got to know Addison… personally." Allen lets out a hard chuckle, puts his hands on his waist, shakes his head, and begins to pant around the room. He says, "I don't believe what I'm hearing. Do you realize what you're saying to me?" I remind him, "Allen, don't you remember; I tried to tell you, but you wouldn't listen to me! You just kept blowing me off, and suggesting that I might be a little paranoid from the move. I tried to tell Ana also, but she wouldn't listen either. She suggested I see a doctor, but I knew it was real. I knew I wasn't crazy. I hear his voice, and I feel his touches." Allen shouts, "His touches! Are you fucking kidding me, Gayle?" I'm weeping as I continue trying to explain, "He's real Allen. I don't want to hurt you, but now I have to be honest with you. I'm also sexually involved with him. I didn't plan this; it just happened."

He hangs his head low, and asks, "Gayle, did you just tell me that you make love to him?" I'm sobbing uncontrollably, "Yes, I did, Allen, and yes, I do love him." Allen is so hurt; he looks like damaged goods. He lifts his head, and says, "Are you fucking serious? I'm doing everything I can to make a future for the two of us, and you're running around fucking a ghost." He grabs and shakes me, and throws me onto the bed. He climbs on top of me, pins me down by my wrists, and shouts in my face, "You ruin what we have for a fucking ghost! What the hell is wrong with you?" I move my head from side to side, as he shouting in my face. I'm crying and screaming, "I'm sorry! I'm so sorry, Allen." He screams, "You're sorry! You're sorry!" He pulls me up, and shakes me again, but this time, Addison punches him in the face, and Allen falls to the floor, holding his jaw. Addison shouts at him, "Don't you ever put your hands on my woman!" I scream, "Addison, stop. Please, please stop!" Allen jumps up, and starts swinging, trying to hit Addison, but he keeps missing. Addison knocks him down again, but this time Allen, somehow, manages to grab his leg, and pulls him down to the floor. The two of them start rustling, and I all I could hear were blows. The next thing I know, Allen is flung into the wall so hard that there's an indent, and cracks in the wall.

The fight is over, and Allen slowly slides down the wall and onto the floor. I quickly run over to him, "Oh My God! Addison, what have you done? He's not moving! Oh my God! He's not moving!" I shake him, "Allen! Allen wake up! Allen, please wake up!" He's not moving. I run to the phone and dial 9-1-1. Oh my God! How am I going to explain this? The Operator answers. Hysterically, I say, "I need an ambulance! My husband is not moving!" She says, "Ma'am what happened?" I shout, "My husband is not moving!" She asks, "Is he breathing?" I shout, "Barely! Please send someone quickly! Please help!" She says, "Ok ma'am, I'm dispatching someone now. What happened?" I respond,

"I don't know! He was wrestling with an intruder… Oh, please get someone here right away! He's not moving!" She says, "Ma'am, please calm down, and try to tell me exactly what happened." I abruptly hang up the phone, and I scream out at Addison, "Look what you've done! Whyyy? You promised me! You promised me!" I'm rocking Allen in my arms, and sobbing profusely.

I'm pacing back and forth, trying to calm myself before the police and paramedics arrive. "Oh My Goodness! What will I tell the police? How am I going to explain this?" I run downstairs, and open the Terrace doors to make it appear to be a burglary. The doorbell rings, and I rush to open the door. I didn't give them a chance to speak, "He's upstairs in the first bedroom! Please hurry!" I run upstairs behind them. Allen is still unconscious, and they're trying to revive him. The officer asks, "Ma'am, what happened?" I explain, "My husband and I were in bed, and this man came into our bedroom from nowhere. They started fighting, and he threw my husband into the wall." I point to the indentation in the wall, and I continue, "I started screaming, and he ran out." The paramedic exclaims, "We're going to have to take him to the hospital." I screech, "What! Oh my God! Will he be okay?" He says, "Ma'am, we need to get him there quickly." I ask, "Where's the hospital? We just moved here, and I don't know my way around yet. How do I get there?" The paramedic says, "Just follow us, ma'am." They hook him up to a ventilator, and roll him out.

I arrive at the hospital, and follow them into the emergency room. They won't let me come into the room, but guide me to the registration desk, to provide Allen's medical information. I'm reluctant, but I go anyway. Afterwards, I'm asked to sit in the waiting area. The officer doesn't waste any time approaching me, to question me about the 'so-called' intruder. I start crying, and explaining, "I didn't see his face; he was wearing a black ski mask. He's about 6'2," with a medium build. That's all I can remember. I don't know how he got in. We didn't hear anything. Everything happened so fast." I'm sobbing, and the officer tries to comfort me, "Its going to be okay, ma'am." After a couple hours, the doctor comes out and says, "He's suffered a mild concussion, but he's going to be alright. He'll be out of it for a while." I ask, "May I see him?" He says, "Yes, but I want him to rest. I'd like to keep him overnight to monitor his progress."

I slowly walk into the room. Allen is lying very still, with his eyes closed. I walk over to the bed, and touch his hand. He slowly opens his eyes, looks up at me, and pulls his hand away. I start crying, "Allen, I'm so sorry. I'm so, so sorry." Tears begin to roll down his face; he closes his eyes, and goes out again. After about an hour, he opens his eyes, and looks over me. His voice is scratched, "Gayle, I'm going to ask you this just once ~ please leave?" I beg, "Allen, please don't ask me to leave. I told the police that it was an intruder, in case they question you." He asks, "So, is that all you're worried about?" I quickly respond, "No! Of course not! I just didn't know what else to tell them. I mean, I couldn't tell them the truth." He asks again, "Gayle, please leave, and don't come back. And, please don't call my parents or anyone else. When I'm ready to talk, I'll contact you." I beg again, "Allen, please! Please don't do this!" He closes his eyes, turns his head, and says, "Goodbye Gayle."

I leave the room sobbing. The police are waiting for me, and one of the officers asks, "Ma'am, will you be going back home tonight?" I answer, "Yes! We're new in town, and I have nowhere else to go." He says, "Well, if you don't mind, we'd like to escort you home, and check things out." I say, "Okay, thank you officer." Then he comments, "It's pretty surprising that a burglary took place in that neighborhood. I mean, we've had a couple of domestic issues, but no burglaries in that area." I sheepishly look up at him, and shake my head.

Chapter Fourteen

Ana's Unsuspecting Comfort

ALLEN PICKS UP the phone, and calls Ana, "I'm sorry to bother you, Ana, but I really need to talk to you, and there's no one else that I can talk to about this shit." She nervously asks, "About what, Allen? What's wrong?" He asks, "Did Gayle just happen to mention some guy named Addison to you?" Ana inhales, "Oh shit! What happened?" Allen is fighting back tears, "I don't even know how to tell you this; Gayle is having an affair with um…" He chokes up, takes a big swallow, and breathes, "She's having an affair, Ana." Ana appears shocked, and asks, "Are you sure, Allen? How do you know?" He bellows out, "Yes, I'm sure! The son of a bitch punched me in the face, we started fighting, and he knocked me unconscious! I'm at General Hospital with a concussion." Ana yells out, "What the hell! Oh My God! Allen, tell me what happened?" He says, "I overheard her having a conversation with this… person, who happens to be a ghost. When I confronted her, she tried to deny that I heard her talking to him, like I was idiot or something. She made me so mad that I grabbed her, threw her on the bed, and started shaking the shit out of her. I know I shouldn't have touched her, Ana, but I was furious, because she just kept lying to me." He takes a breather, and continues, "Then out of nowhere, this… this… thing just punched me, and he slung me into the wall. The scary thing is, he has a physical body, and he talks. Can you imagine trying to defend yourself against someone you can't even see?" Ana is horrified, "Oh my goodness! Allen, I am so sorry. I can't believe what I'm hearing. I can't believe that he actually hit you." He says, "I know! Unbelievable, right! But, you haven't heard anything yet! She told me that she was having an affair with this guy, that she loves him, and that she's sexually involved with him." Ana shakes her head in disbelief, "O.M.G! So, it is real!" Allen asks, "Ana, what do you mean, "It is real!" She responds, "Allen, she kept trying to tell me about this, but I thought she was losing it. Oh boy! Where is Gayle now?" He says, "I could care less. I couldn't look at her without being disgusted, so I sent her home or wherever. She probably went back to him. Who knows?" Ana says, "Allen, I'm on my way up to the hospital." He says, "Ana, you don't have to come here; you're just the only person I can talk to about this." She says, "I know, Allen, and that's why I'm on my way. I'll see you shortly."

Ana comes into Allen's room, he turns his head towards her, and tears start streaming down his face. He looks pitiful, and pretty beat up. She lets out a heavy sigh, and gives him a big hug. He starts crying even harder, and says, "Ana, I feel stupid, and so embarrassed, telling you this shit." Ana says, "Its okay, Allen; I witnessed some of it at the party." He yells, "What!" She affirms, "I couldn't believe what I was hearing, or seeing. It's just too bizarre to even comprehend. I mean, it's like something out of a movie or something. This shit doesn't really happen in real life ~ at least, that's what I thought. Honestly, Allen, I don't know exactly how to respond to this; it's too preposterous." Allen shakes his head, "I know, Ana." Ana sympathetically says, "I feel so bad, Allen. Gayle, tried to tell me a few times, but I didn't believe her. I told her that she needed to see a doctor. As close as she and I are, I should have known that she wouldn't just make this up. She had no one else to confide in, so she started a relationship with him. Oh My God! I feel partially responsible. I'm her best friend, and I rejected her. I can't believe this is actually happening." He shouts, "You! You can't even remotely imagine how or what I feel, Ana! What am I supposed to do? Hell, Ana, he's a fucking Ghost! Man, I thought this kind of shit only happened in the movies. This is all my fault; I'm the one who should have listened to her. And, now she's all caught up. I mean, she's in love with this… this freak!"

    Allen divulges what he witnessed. "Ana, I caught them fucking in 'my' bed. I feel like a damn fool; I thought she was dreaming about us, when all the time, I'm watching her make love to him." He hits the bed, "Damn! Damn! Damn!" Ana says, "Calm down Allen. Calm down. I know you love her, and I know she loves you. She needs us, Allen. She's caught between two worlds, and she doesn't know how to get out, but somehow, we've got to help her." Allen shouts, "Help her! Are you kidding! I'm the one bruised, both physically and emotionally. I did nothing but love her, and she's having an affair right under my nose, in my house, and in my bed!" Ana says, "Allen, you know that Gayle would never 'deliberately' cheat on you." He retorts, "Well, Ana, what would call having sex with someone outside of your marriage?" Ana says nothing, but her expression says it all. Allen observes Ana's countenance and says, "That's what I thought!"

    Ana says, "Okay, let's talk this out. She tried to tell us that something was going on in that house, but we [that's you and me] did not listen to her. We both patronized her, made her feel insecure, and helpless. She had no one else to talk with about something so scandalous, and she had nowhere to go. All she had was him, and he took full advantage of the situation. She was vulnerable, and she was trapped, and he seduced her. We failed her [period]! And now, we've got to help her. You, especially, cannot just give up on her." He shouts, "Help her! Help her! Are you fucking kidding me? She didn't look like she wanted to be rescued when she was fucking the shit out of him!" Ana calmly says, "Allen, she was pleading for our help, and we didn't help her. You've got to forgive her." Allen begins to cry again, "I know, Ana, but I don't know how. I don't know what to do. Hell, this guy is living in our home, or should I say, we're living in his home." Ana looks over at him, "Well, maybe you need to make it 'NOT' your home anymore." Allen is quiet for a moment, and then he looks at Ana like a light bulb just lit up in his head. He then nods, and says, "That's it, Ana! I think you may have given me half the solution. It's time to move, but first I've got to emotionally get pass this. I mean, I can't just forgive and forget... not just like that. But, thank you for helping me through this; I appreciate you so much. I love you Sis." Ana smiles, and says, "That's what I'm here for. We need each other."

Ana gets up to leave, and deeply sighs, "Well, what's your next step, Allen?" He says, "I don't know yet; I need to think things through. I really need to clear my head, but thank you again, Ana." She says, "Okay, but if you need to talk more, just call me." She gives him a big hug, and he caresses her tightly, and begins sobbing again. She tries to comfort him, and gently palms his face, and looks into his eyes, "It's going to be okay, Allen. We're going to get through this together. You hear me?" She begins to whimper, he pulls her close to comfort her, and now they're face to face, crying together. Allen pulls her even closer, and kisses her lips. Ana is startled, but then she reciprocates. They kiss long and hard, and now they're both fully aroused. Allen unbuttons her blouse, and starts sucking her breasts. Ana, frantically, raises her skirt, takes off her shoes, and climbs on top of him. Her heart is pounding, and she's breathing heavy. She feels his hard prick touching her wet pussy. She whispers, "Oh, Allen (as she's trying to catch her breath)... What are we doing?" He says, "Shhh..." He pulls his erect penis from his underwear, and quickly penetrates her pussy. Ana lets out a loud squeal, with tears of fulfillment falling down her cheeks, and then she starts riding his shank. She yells, "Oh my goodness! Oh my goodness! I'm sorry, Allen; it's been a long time since I've been fucked, and I'm about to cum already." He starts bucking faster, "Come on baby! Come on baby! Give daddy some sweet honey." She lets out a loud yelp, weakens, and falls to his chest, but he's not finished yet. He continues to buck, until he cracks his nuts. He lets out a load moan, and then it was over. Ana climbs out of the bed, pulls down her skirt, and puts on her shoes. Allen wipes his penis down with the sheets, and Ana just stands there. They stare at each other [in silence], with deep penitence, and then she shouts, "Oh My God! Allen, this was a big mistake! This was a big, big mistake!" He concurs, "You're right, Ana, and I'm so sorry. How could we have let this happen? I love my wife, and I know you love her also." Ana agrees, "I know you love Gayle, and you know I love her too. I'm so sorry; we went too far, and this can never, and I mean NEVER, happen again. Gayle can never find out about this." He agrees, "You're right, Ana; this would crush her." Ana is now feeling guilty, but also satisfied. She picks up her purse to exit, but turns around and says, "How could we dare judge Gayle after what just took place. Look at us, Allen; we're pathetic." She swiftly walks out the door, with tears streaming down her face. Allen turns on his side and begins to sob profusely, "What the fuck was I thinking?"

Ana gets into her car, and just bawls her eyes out. She's talking to herself, "I can't believe what I just did! Oh God! Please forgive me." She's in a daze, and shouts "What was I thinking? Hell! What was he thinking?" Although she is truly sorry, she's always had a secret admiration for Allen. Gayle was always flaunting, and talking about how wonderful he was in bed, but Ana dared not ever cross those lines ~ until now. She loves Gayle way too much. Her cell phone rings; it's Allen. He says, "Ana, I just want to apologize again. I was hurting, and wanted some comfort, but that was not the way to get it. Please forgive me; I know I crossed the line." She responds, "I forgive you, Allen, but I must apologize also. I reciprocated, which makes me at fault also." He says, "Well, let's just let bygones be bygones." Ana says, "Agreed! Good night, Allen."

Ana is guilt-ridden, "Well, that's what you call, putting a Band-Aid on it! Now, how are we going to fix this? I'm judging Gayle, but I'm even worse than she is. If Allen and I were anywhere but the hospital, I might have fucked him all night. He's so fine and refined, and I've always wondered, but I knew that he was definitely 'hands-off.' I can't believe what just happened." Ana screams to the top of her lungs, "THIS IS MY BEST FRIEND'S HUSDAND! What have I done? I'm supposed to be focused on trying to help my best friend, but I'm sitting here thinking about fucking her husband. I'm the one who needs to see a doctor. How can I possibly face her now? I need a drink."

Chapter Fifteen

Look What You've Done!

I UNLOCK THE door, and the police go inside to search the place. They insist that I wait outside with another officer until they've thoroughly checked the house. The police finish their search, and give me the clear to enter. The officer says, "The intruder must've have come in through the Terrace doors, as they were left wide open." I act surprised and say, "What! Oh my goodness! We had a party last night, and we must've forgotten to lock the Terrace doors." The officer says, "Not to worry, we've lock things up, and checked all the windows and doors. But, if you're going to stay here, please put the alarm on." I say, "Thank you, officers," and they leave.

I slowly look around, and boy, I'm boiling on the inside. I stand with my arms crossed, looking around for signs of Addison. I'm so furious with him, that I can spit. He doesn't say a word, and I shout out, "Addison! Where the hell are you?" Surprisingly, he says, "I'm right here, Gayle. You don't have to shout." I yell, "How could you? You could have killed my husband!" He says, "He was hurting you, and I couldn't let that happen." I yell at him, "Addison, if you would have just kept your composure, and even stayed away when Allen and I were together, this would have never happened! But nooo... you've been trying to reveal your existence for some time now. Well, now you've done it! You've blown it! You've messed up big time!" Addison says, "Gayle, please listen to me." I shout at him, "Addison, there is nothing I want, or need to hear from you! All of this is your fault! Just leave me alone!" I go upstairs, slam my bedroom door, lie across the bed, and just bawl.

Addison sits on the bed and rubs my back, "I apologize, Gayle. Will you ever forgive me?" I ask, "Why did you have to hit him, Addison? What were you thinking? I'm so mad at you right now." Addison tries to defend his actions again, "Because of the way he was grabbing on you, and pushing you around. How could I just do nothing?" I yell at him, "Allen would never hurt me, Addison!" He yells back, "Well, he could have fooled me, Gayle! He was pretty enraged, and you never know what a person that angry is capable of." I blurt out, "Do you blame him? I mean, I'm having an affair, he catches me talking to my lover, and I flat out deny it, trying to make him look like he's the one with the problem." Addison says, "That's no excuse for him to put his hands on you, Gayle!" I say, "Come on, Addison! I have to take some of the blame. I hurt him." He says, "Its okay, Gayle, I love you." I tell him, "I love you too, Addison, but I also love my husband, and now I don't know what's going to happen. I don't know if he's going to leave me or…" Addison interrupts, "So what if he does? You won't have to worry. I'll be here for you. Then it would be just us ~ alone. I can make you happy, Gayle." I bellow out, "Are you serious, Addison? I love Allen, and I don't want to lose him. How could you possibly think that you can make me happy? Addison, you're a ghost. You're not even supposed to be here. You can't support me financially! You can't even leave this house, which means we never go out for walks, out to dinner, to the movies or anywhere." He says, "Gayle, please just give us a chance. You don't know what the future holds for the two of us." I shout, "Future! Future! Can't you see, Addison, there could be no future for us! Oh My God! What was I thinking? Lord please, bring my husband back to me." Addison says, "What about us, Gayle?" I say, "What about us, Addison? I'm sorry, and I don't mean to be cruel, but I want my husband - a man that I can see, take strolls with, go out to dinner with, have kids with..." I'm sobbing even louder, "I just want my husband!"

He arrogantly says, "So you were just using me? I was there for you when your husband wasn't. All he cared about was work and making money, but I was the one here for you. I made you feel good all the time. I made you laugh. I made you happy. I made the best love to you that you've ever had, and you said so yourself." Addison is angry, and he starts picking up things, and throwing them around the room. I'm scared. "I wasn't using you, Addison. Remember, you pursued me, and not the other way around. And yes, you did make me feel special and, yes, I do love you, Addison; but I love, and I need my husband." I pick up my purse to leave, and he yells, "Where do you think you're going?" I tell him, "I'm going to see my husband!" Addison slams the door shut to keep me from leaving. He grabs my arm, and he's angry, "No, you're not going anywhere right now! We're not finished talking!" I respond, "Addison, there's no need to talk anymore. We made a huge mistake, and I've got to see my husband, and plead for his forgiveness. I've got to fix this." I jerk my arm away from his grip and say, "I guess you're going to push me around also, huh?" He says, "No, I wouldn't do that, Gayle, but I need to know what's going to happen with us?" I say, "I'm sorry Addison; there is no us." He says, "Just like that?" I open the door, "I'm sorry, Addison, but it will have to be 'just like that'. I run downstairs, out to the garage, and into my car. I didn't know where I was going. I just had to leave that house, as I didn't feel like contending with Addison all night. I check into a hotel, and I cry myself to sleep.

Chapter Sixteen

Allen Is Released . . . Now what?

I SLEPT LATER than usual, and I immediately jump up and call the hospital. Allen's nurse said that he was ready to be released; they just need to have the release papers drawn up for signature. I quickly shower, and head up to the hospital to pick him up. I walk into his room, and he's sitting on the edge of the bed. I run over to him, pleading, "Allen, I'm so sorry. I'm so, so sorry. I don't know what I was thinking. I beg you to please forgive me. I don't want to lose you. I love you too much." The nurse comes into the room with the release papers. He signs them, and the nurse says, "You're free to go."

Allen is remorseful, and he knows that he can't be too hard on Gayle after what just took place with him and Ana. We get in the car, and I head back to the hotel. Allen asks, "Where are we going, Gayle?" I tell him, "I stayed at this hotel last night. I couldn't stay at the house after what happened." There's a moment of silence, then he speaks, "Gayle, I really don't know how to respond. I don't know what to say. I'm confused. I'm hurt. I'm shocked. This is so fucking unnatural! We can't even go to a counselor with this bizarre shit. Who would ever believe it? If Ana hadn't seen the two of you rendezvousing at the party, she wouldn't have believed it either." Surprised, I say, "Ana! You've talked to Ana?" He says, "Yes, I called her, and she came up to the hospital last night. I mean, who else could I talk with about this shit? If I hadn't witnessed it for myself, I wouldn't have believe it. I'm still baffled. This feels like something out of the twilight zone. How do I get pass this?" I say, "Allen, I want you to know that I would never just go out and deliberately cheat on you. I made a big mistake, and I'm asking you to please forgive me." Allen sighs, but doesn't say a word. I continue, "I tried to tell you and Ana what I was hearing and feeling, but neither of you would listen to me. I couldn't tell anyone else, and I didn't know what else to do. He wouldn't leave me alone, and I had nowhere else to go. I was trapped in my own home. I'm so sorry, Allen."

Allen looks at me with sorrow in his eyes, "Gayle, I know this is partially my fault, and it was bound to happen. I'm working all these long hours, and not spending enough time with you. You're alone too much, and I'm sorry. I know I drove you to this point." I dispute his claim, "No! You're not hearing me! This had nothing to do with you not being at home, but everything to do with you not listening to me. I felt like I had no choice, because no one was hearing me!" He responds, "You're right! You're right! I should have listened to you, but instead, I mocked you. Can you ever forgive me? This could have all been avoided if I would have just listened to you." He shakes his head, and sighs, "I'm so sorry, Gayle. I love you, but I have to confess, this is a really hard pill to swallow, and it's going to take some time to bring total restoration to this relationship." His words give me hope, and I'm feeling a sense of reprieve. I say, "I know Allen, but we can get pass it. I don't care what we have to do." He says, "Well, for starters, if we're going to make this work, the first thing we'll have to do is move.

I refuse to stay in that house with that freak another night." I agree, "Okay, Allen, let's move. Anywhere you say, I'll go."

I lean over to kiss him, but he turns his head and says, "I'm not quite ready for that yet." I nod and say, "I understand." Then I look over at him and ask, "Is it okay if we stop by the house, grab some of our belongings, and then head back to the hotel?" He gives me this blank stare, and then says, "Okay, but just long enough to get what we need, and then we're leaving out right away. I don't want another encounter with that freak." I nod in agreement. He says, "We'll stay at the hotel until we find another home. I'll call off tomorrow, and we can start looking right away."

We enter the house, and Allen is cautiously looking around, and so am I. It's quiet, but I know Addison is near. We quickly grab some personal necessities, and make our way back downstairs. Addison asks, "So where are the two of you going?" Allen and I are both startled, and I blurt out, "We're leaving here!" Addison questions us again, "What do you mean, leaving here?" Allen speaks up, "Just what she said, we're leaving here! Now, you can haunt this place all by your damn self. You're not even supposed to be here. You really need to cross over, and find some peace, but it won't be with my wife anymore." Addison pompously retorts, "For your information, man, your wife happens to enjoy my company." I speak up, "But, that didn't make it right, Addison! I love my husband, and I'm going to be with my husband. Being with you was a big mistake." Addison adds salt to the wound, "So, you're saying all love-making we shared everyday was a big mistake?" I blurt out, "Yes!" I know Addison was just trying to provoke Allen to anger. But not this time; Allen keeps his cool, and we continue making our way to the door. Allen and I leave out through the garage, drive away, and head to the hotel.

The rest of the day, Allen is very quiet, not saying much of anything. We get into bed, and he moves to the opposite end of the bed. I move close to him, and caress his arm. He pulls away and says, "I'm sorry, Gayle, but I'm just not there yet." I move back to the other side of the bed and mutter, "I understand."

I wake up in the middle of the night, and hear Allen weeping. I feel awful, but I don't want to bother him, so I pretend that I'm still asleep. I hear him whisper to himself, "What have I done? Why didn't I exercise more self-control? I'm so ashamed." I'm thinking to myself, "What is he talking about? It's not his fault. I'm the one who should have exercised more self-control. I'm the one who should be ashamed."

We rise early, and our eyes are red and swollen from crying all night. I'm so sorry to make him feel this way. I'm wondering, "Can this ever be fixed? Will he ever truly forgive me? Will he ever trust me again?" But, I'm also thinking to myself, "How could something so good to you, be so bad for you? If Addison would have just kept his cool, this could have been 'our' secret." If the truth be told, the only reason for my sorrow is because I got caught. Other than that, I'm not regretful. I love Addison, and what we shared was exhilarating; it was refreshing, but now it's over.

Things are pretty solemn between Allen and me this morning. We're both perusing the internet, looking for a home. After a while, we find several houses that we're both anxious to see, so we call a Realtor to schedule the showings. The Realtor is going to call us back with confirmations. In the interim, Allen calls his secretary to inform her that he will not be in the office today, and to reschedule his appointments. We stop in the café, and take advantage of the hotel's continental breakfast, but things are still pretty dry between us, just some small talk. My cell phone rings, and it's the Realtor informing us that we're confirmed to see four of the houses we chose, and where to meet her. Prior to us meeting with the Broker, we stop by the management company to put our house up for sub-lease, starting immediately. I know that there's going to be a hoard of people calling to get it. It's much too nice to stay empty for too long. We looked at some beautiful houses, and each house that we viewed, Allen inquired about its history. I think he may be a little paranoid, after the Addison ordeal. After several hours of viewing houses, we choose one that we both love. We sign the required documents, and have to wait a couple days for the response.

Chapter Seventeen

The Orchestrated Lessee

IT'S BEEN A couple days, and Allen still hasn't loosened up as much as I'd hope, but we've had a few chuckles, here and there. I know that it's going to take some time, and I'm willing to patiently wait. We finally get the 'Approval' to move into our new place this weekend, so we met with the movers, and gave them the instructions to pack and move everything to our new home. Everything is all set, except the sub-leasing of our existing home. Allen asks, "Will you be okay handling the showings for the house." I shrug my shoulders, "Yeah; I'm okay with it. I'll take care of everything." He says, "Good, because I don't ever want to step foot in that house again. But, I want to make sure that you're comfortable going back in there." I respond, "I believe I'll be okay." Allen is trusting me, and I don't want to blow it again, although I don't know how I'll react hearing Addison's voice, after all that's taken place. Allen says, "I'll contact Bill and let him know that we've found a place, and are moving this weekend."

We meet back at the hotel, and my cell phone is ringing off the hook. People are calling to inquire about the sublet. So far, I've got two appointments scheduled for Monday morning - Mr. and Mrs. Frank Rodgers at 10:00, and a Melody Hopkins at 11:00. I just want to get this done and over with, so my life can get back to normal ~ whatever that is.

Well, we're all moved into our new place. It's as beautiful as the other house, but it's not as big. We spent the entire weekend, unpacking and getting settled. Allen appears to pretty content with the house, and so am I. It's Monday morning. Allen heads to the office, and I'm on my way to the house for the showings. Mr. and Mrs. Rodgers pull up in the driveway at the same time as I do. We get out of our respective cars, and greet one another. Mrs. Rodgers says, "We drove by the house yesterday, and peeped in through the windows. It is absolutely lovely. Why did you move?" I tell her, "Because my husband wanted to be closer to his job." I open the door, and they are just in awe. I tell them, "Please take your time, and if you have any questions, just yell out for me. I'll be out on the Terrace." I'm thinking about how much I'm going to miss this place.

I stand out on the Terrace, the wind is softly blowing through my hair, and the tears are streaming down my cheeks. I'm really going to miss this place. Addison softly wipes away my tears and says, "Please don't cry, Gayle. Please don't cry." I'm so glad to hear his voice, I feel around for him, and squeeze him so tight, "Ohhh Addison! I'm going to miss you so much. My heart is aching right now." He starts crying, "What am I going to do without you, Gayle?" I just close my eyes, and rest my head on his chest. I painfully say, "Please hold me, Addison." He holds me close, and we stand there embracing each other. I don't want to let him go.

Mr. Rodgers clears his throat and asks, "Are you alright?" Embarrassed, I giggle, "I'm in a play, and I thought I'd rehearse my lines while you were looking through the house." He and Mrs. Rodgers give a slight giggle and he says, "You sure sounded convincing to us." I say, "Thank you! I appreciate that." Mr. Rodgers says, "Well, we love the house, but we've got a couple more houses to see. We'll definitely get back to you with our intentions. Thank you for letting us see it." I thanked them for coming, and escorted them out the front door.

Addison blurts out, "I hope they don't come back; I don't like them." I strike at him, "Whatever Addison! They are a nice couple." He says, "I know, Gayle, but they are not you." The doorbell rings, and I tell him, "Well, here's our next showing. Her name is Melody Hopkins." He says, "Hum, she's a homely looking thing, isn't she?" I sigh and laugh, "Shhh…she might hear you." I open the door, and Melody and I greet each other.

Melody is a drab-looking lady in her mid-thirties, with thick glasses, hair pulled back in a tight bun, long black skirt, a white ruffled blouse, and black winter tights.

She steps into the foyer and gasps, "Oh my! This place is more beautiful than I expected." I smile and say, "I'm glad you like it, Melody. Please take your time, and peruse through the place." She says, "It's so lovely. Why are you moving?" I reply, "My husband didn't like the long commute to work, so we found another lovely place closer to his office." She smiles and says, "I completely understand." I tell her, "Take your time, and if you need me, I'll be out on the Terrace."

Addison says, "Urggg… What a bore. She's a true nerd!" I chuckle, "But, she appears to be a nice lady, Addison." He remarks, "Yeah, okay!" I comment, "I just can't believe it; it's nearly 90 degrees, and she's wearing thick black tights, and winter shoes." He comments, "I told you she was a nerd, and I don't like her either." I jokingly say, "You never knooow." He seriously says, "Oh no! I do know, and she's not it.

There will never be another you, Gayle." I breathe deeply, "I'm sorry, Addison. This is hard for both of us." He asks, "Do you think you'll ever come back to visit me?" I respond, "No! I can't. I'm really trying to get my marriage back on track." He affectionately kisses me, "I love you so much, Gayle." I reciprocate, "I love you more, Addison." He pleads, "Gayle, please don't just leave me like this. What am I supposed to do?" I respond, "Addison, I never would have left you. You did this to us." He starts crying, "I know, and I'm so sorry."

Melody softly asks, "Is it okay to come out on the Terrace?" I respond, "Of course it's okay." She says, "Oh! I heard you talking on the phone, and I didn't want to interrupt you. This place is beautiful; when will it be available?" I reply, "It's available now." She gets excited, and exclaims, "I want it!" I chuckle, "Okay, then you can have it, if everything checks out." I then ask, "Do you have family moving in with you?" She responds, "No. It's just me, and my work. I'm too busy to even think about anybody else. However, it is getting a little old, and sometimes I do get a little lonely." We walk back inside and I ask, "Melody, if you don't mind me asking, what do you do?" She says, "I'm an Architect." Surprised, I say, "Really! The guy who designed and built this home is an Architect. I heard he's a beautiful soul. Perhaps, you'll get to meet him one day." She says, "I surely hope so; I'd love to compliment him on this masterpiece." I smile, "I'm sure he'll love that, Melody. I happen to love everything about this house, and I'm almost certain that you'll feel the same way. It kind of rubs on you just the right way." I smile at Addison, as I knew he was very near. Melody asks, "Do you mind if I walk through one more time?" I gesture for her to go ahead.

I whisper to Addison, "See now! The two of you already have something in common. She's an Architect." He says, "Yeah, right! She's not my type, Gayle. Look at her!" Melody reappears and reiterates, "I want it! What do I need to do to get started?" Excitedly, I say, "Oh, great! I think this house will be perfect for you. Meet me tomorrow morning at 11:00 a.m. at the management office, on the corner of Oak and Grand. We'll get all the necessary docs completed, and after they've verified everything, they'll give us a call. It's that simple!" She says, "I know exactly where that is. I'll see you tomorrow morning, Gayle." I walk her to the front door, we shake hands, and she leaves. Addison sighs, "Wow! That was quick!" I respond, "I knew it would be, Addison. Who wouldn't just adore this place? You see how people react when they enter the foyer. Everyone is awed by your work."

Chapter Eighteen

One Last Time . . . Our Forever Secret

SUDDENLY, IT ALL just hits me, and I start sobbing profusely, "Addison, I'm really going to miss you." He embraces me, "I'm going to miss the hell out of you too, Gayle." He grabs me close, and thrusts his tongue deep into my mouth. I can feel my underwear getting drenched with the secretion from my vagina. I take off my panties, and he inserts his fingers into my pussy. Ohhh... my sweet sticky fluids are creeping down my thighs. He kneels down, and licks up all my sweetness. Oh la la... I go down on my knees, and feel for his penis. Its bone hard, and I need to taste it. I need to feel it in my mouth. I'm stroking it with my hand, and he's moaning ever so loudly. He lies prostrate, I bend down, and begin sucking him off. He grabs my hair, and pulls my head back, as he about to bust a nut. I can feel his dick, swelling and hardening between my jaws. Suddenly, he just howls out, and lets loose. My pussy is pumping, and I need some dick. I start kissing and caressing his body, and he's just moaning in pleasure. I feel his penis rising again, and I massage the head of it, in and around my pussy hole, enticing him to fuck me. He swiftly flips me over, and plunges his hard prick deep into my beckoning vagina. I can't hold back any longer, and I cum right away. He's still pumping, and I'm still pulsating. I'm so doused in my own wetness, that the vibrating of his penis, moving in, out and deep, is driving me absolutely nuts. I scream out in utter contentment, as I'm cumming again. And, he cums right behind me. He falls on me, and begins crying hard. I start crying also; I can't stand the pain. It feels like someone took a hammer and shattered my heart into little pieces. He says, "Oh Gayle, I hate myself for what I've done to us."

My cell phone rings, and I jump up to answer it; it's Allen. "Hey Honey." He happily responds, "Hey Babe. How were the showings?" I lie and say, "Well, Melody is still here, and I think she wants the place." He says, "Great! Good job, Honey!" I tell him, "She's walking through it for a second time, and that's a good sign." He asks, "Hey, is there any sign of You-Know-Who?" I respond, "Well, when I first came in, he spoke and let me know that he's not going to bother me, and so far, so good. I haven't heard a peep from him." I could hear the relief in his tone, "That's good, Honey. Well, finish up, and I'll see you a little later." I say, "Okay. Love you!" He says, "I love you too, Gayle." I thought I'd feel guilty for lying to him, but I didn't. I wanted this time with Addison. This was our finale, and I needed this closure.

I lie back in Addison's arms. It feels so good, and it feels so natural, although I know it's wrong. I want to be with this man, but I know I can't, so I'll just relish this moment. I say, "Addison, I have to confess that I'm a little envious about Melody moving in here." He sputters, "I don't know why!" I say, "You know you 'can' be a little irresistible." He blurts out, "Yeah, but you don't ever have to worry about me touching her. She's definitely not my type." I say, "You never know… never say never."

After a moment of just lying in his arms, I tell him, "Addison, I'd better be going. I don't want Allen to get suspicious." He says, "I understand, Gayle. But, you know I hate to see you leave me. It feels like the end of the world." We take a quick shower together, and he shouts out, "Damn it! I'm going to miss this! I'm going to miss you, woman!" I pull him close, and I can't stop the tears from flowing. "I'm going to miss you too, Addison." He says, "So this is it?" I say, "Yes! This is it, Babe!" We get out the shower, he grabs the bath towel, and pats my body dry. I get dressed, and he walks me downstairs to the door.

I feel bad about leaving him. And, I'm almost glad that I can't see him, because this would be even harder. He gives a feeble laugh, "Too bad I can't keep you in a bottle, and call you out when I want or need you." I sadly say, "Good bye, Addison; I'll always love you!" He sniffles, "I'll always love you too, Gayle." I painfully walk out, and lock up the house. On the way home, I'm sobbing profusely. You want something so bad that it hurts, but you know you can't have it. It's a different type of agony, and I'm not sure if it ever goes away - Time will tell.

I come home, and Allen hasn't arrived yet. I sigh in relief because it's obvious that I've been crying, as my eyes are swollen and red, and my makeup is smeared. And, the last thing I need is for Allen to start asking me questions. When he did come in, I had to pretend that I was really excited about subletting the house. He was happy, and wanted to celebrate. Although we weren't there yet, I was praying that he didn't want to make love, because this little va-jay-jay of mine was 'out of commission.' But, I was a little nervous, because I wasn't sure if he would want to make love to me, just to see if I had been with Addison. Whew! Thank goodness he didn't.

Allen is coming around slowly, but it's been a few weeks and we still haven't made love. He keeps saying that he's "still not there yet," but damn, how long will it take? And even though he kisses me; it's not the same either. Ana said, "Baby steps." But how long is "baby steps?" I guess it's easy for me to say; I'm the one who messed up. Allen and I dare not mention Addison's name, but I think about him on a regular basis. "What is he doing? How are things with him and Melody? Does he miss me?" Honestly, I still miss him, but I know it'll eventually wear off, especially once Allen and I hit the sheets again. Poor Melody; I bet he completely ignores her. I shake my head, "Boy, if Addison would have just kept his cool…Wow!"

Chapter Nineteen

Who's That Lady?
No, It Couldn't Be . . .

A COUPLE MONTHS after the move, Ana and I are dining outside at a café in Chicago. We hadn't talked about Addison in a while. All that was said, was said, and pretty much left in the past. She did, however, apologize to me for not being there for me when I needed her the most. I, sincerely, accepted her apology. I'm not sure how I would have reacted if she or anyone else would have told me such a story, but I do know now that I can't confide in her about everything. Some things are just not meant to be told.

There's something different about Ana though. She's been a little distant with me. I know it's going to take her a while to get over all that happened, but it's not like I did anything to her. I don't know why she's been so vague with me. The funny thing is, she rarely even mentions Allen's name. I guess she still feels sorry for him. I can't believe that she still hasn't come to see the new house either. She says that she's been pretty busy. All is well between us though. We're slowly trying to get back on track.

We had just finished our meal, and this stunning young woman is walking towards us. I didn't recognize her, but apparently she recognized me. She's looking flawlessly beautiful. She's wearing a sexy little halter dress, her hair is flowing softly, she's bare-legged, and wearing sexy sandals. She stops by our table and excitedly says, "Gayle! Oh my God! It's so good to see you!" Of course, I'm stunned, "Oh my goodness, Melody, is that you? How are you?" I introduce her to Ana. They smile and shake hands. I say, "I didn't recognize you without your glasses, and with your hair down. It's like a brand new you." She says, "I know, everyone is saying the same thing. I'm just feeling so free these days. I've never felt so sexy and alive in all my life."

I'm refraining from laughter, "Wow! That's great! Does moving into the house have anything to do with it?" She has this sexy smirk-like smile, "Oh yeah. It has everything to do with it. You told me that I'd love everything about this house, and you were right; this house rubs you just the right way." I say, "Wow! That's so good to hear, Melody." I'm lying through my teeth; that's the last thing I wanted to hear. I say, "I'm glad you love it, Melody." But now, I'm a little curious so I ask, "Did you ever get a chance to meet the architect that built the house? I hear he lives somewhere in town. Too bad, I never got a chance to personally meet him. I would have loved to compliment him personally." She says, "Oh yeah, we did meet. He's such an awesome guy, with so many talents. And, yes, he does live in town. In fact, he lives in close proximity. We've talked for hours, and he's taught me things that I never even dreamed of." Then she looks down at her watch and says, "Oh, I need to hurry home, Gayle, I've been gone all day, and I've got to catch up on some things." I'm thinking to myself, "I just bet you do." I say, "Okay, Melody. It's so good to see you." She says, "Ana, it's nice to meet you." Ana smiles and nods, "Likewise, Melody." I yell out, "Hey Melody! If you ever get a chance to talk with that Architect again, please tell him that I loved living in his home." She says, "Okay! I'll be sure to tell him."

She continued sashaying happily down the street, swinging her purse. Ana and I look at each other and burst into laughter. Although, I am happy to be with my husband, I do wonder if Addison ever thinks of me, especially since Melody is at the house. Oh well, now we all have a happy-ever-after ending...

CPSIA information can be obtained
at www.ICGtesting.com
Printed in the USA
LVOW12s1117121016
508418LV00021B/83/P